THE FAE DEALINGS

A DRAGON-MYTH CYCLE PREQUEL

JOSEPH FINLEY

TARASTONE PRESS

I

THE MISSION

1

A HISS IN THE WIND

A half-hour before dawn, Maugis d'Aygremont, chief counselor to the King, crept like a thief through the back alleyways of Paris. Rats scurried away as he skirted around trails of sewage that ran down the cramped alleys. He was careful to avoid leaving footprints that might mark his path. No one had seen him slip away from the old Roman fortress that served as the King's palace when the royal court was visiting the city. And the only three members of the court who knew the purpose of his undertaking were waiting for him at the wharves.

As he turned down another passage in the maze of back alleys that wound through the taverns, storefronts, and homes packed onto the Île-de-la-Cité, his breath froze in the brisk air—and so did his muscles, the moment he heard footfalls at the end of the alleyway.

Two men emerged, a pair of dark silhouettes between the facades of frame houses that leaned into the alley. One of the two looked as burley as a blacksmith; the other stood tall and lanky while a trace of moonlight glinted off the dagger in his hand. "We wants what's in the bag," the lanky man said with a rasp in his voice.

Maugis brushed his right hand over the satchel slung across his shoulder. It held his most precious possession, a leather-bound book that recorded the arcane secrets he had spent his adult life discovering. His fingers drifted from the satchel to the hilt of his sword hidden behind the old traveler's cloak he wore. In his left hand, he gripped his quarterstaff made of hard ash and blackened with soot and flaxseed oil, making it blend into the shadows that fell off the eaves of the houses flanking the alleyway. The men might not have even realized he was holding the staff. Yet now they had seen him, and Maugis could not afford to be seen.

"You want my satchel," he told them, "then come and get it."

"Don't mind if we do," the lanky man replied, stepping into the alley. Beside him, his burly partner hefted a club adorned with jagged iron spikes, but both stopped moving when they spied the quarterstaff. The lanky man flashed a mirthless smile. "Why don't you just put that down and hand over the bag?"

If he had been around an open flame, Maugis would have shown them what his staff could do. But he needed to draw them closer, so he dropped the staff and let it clatter onto the cobblestones. Then he slowly unslung the satchel from his shoulder and held it out with his left hand.

The lanky man cast a wary glance to his partner, who answered with a cruel nod. The lanky man grinned back, revealing a mouthful of rotten teeth. "Good boy," he said, reaching for the satchel.

Maugis waited until the man leaned in before ripping his sword from its scabbard. It was not a typical longsword used by the King's finest warriors but rather was short with a leaf-shaped blade. The sword had a use far beyond physical combat, though its edge was razor sharp and it cleaved through the muscles of the lanky man's arm, right below the elbow.

The lanky man wailed, dropping his dagger as his right hand flew to the bloody wound on his left arm. With one man disarmed, Maugis spun toward the other and sliced his sword across the man's chest. The burly man fell back a step. The cut from the blade had torn through a leather breastplate but had not reached flesh. Still, both men stared at Maugis with slackened jaws. The old traveler's cloak had fallen behind his shoulder, revealing his hauberk of mail polished to a silver sheen.

"Holy hell, Grimoald," the lanky man snapped at his partner. "You didn't tell me he was one of the twelve!"

The burly man barked back like a quarreling lover. "The Blackbird never said nothing about that! Just get the satchel he said, and kill 'im if you can."

The lanky man grimaced. "Then *kill* him!"

With his club raised over his head, the burly man let out a yell and charged. In the split second before the man reached him, Maugis realized for the first time that these two were more than just common thieves. Someone had hired them to find him, which meant someone knew of the mission. But there was no time to ponder that now. In a reaction born from years of training, Maugis dropped the satchel and darted to his left as the club whooshed past him. The burly man had put all of his strength into that strike, and the momentum sent him careening forward. It was a desperate and reckless move, and Maugis made him pay for it, whipping his blade into the back of the man's thigh until it struck bone. Howling in pain, the burly man lurched back with a wild swing of his spiked club. With the flat of his blade, Maugis knocked away the blow and then thrust the tip of his sword through the man's throat. Maugis yanked the blade free and watched as the burly man slumped onto the cobblestones, blood gurgling from the mortal wound. But a patter of footsteps snapped his attention back to the lanky man— who was fleeing down the alley with the satchel clutched in his arms.

Maugis drew a sharp breath. He cleared his thoughts of everything but the words he was about to utter. Words forged from the language of creation and mastered over years of practice and studying. The apothegm Orionde had taught him echoed in his mind as he drew upon the arcane energy needed for this summoning. *Stone cuts earth, staff kindles fire. Sword parts air, cup binds water. Spirit incites the power.* He began moving his sword in a circular motion while he recited the verse. The words were neither Latin nor Greek, but alien in sound with the melody of a song. Around him, the air thrummed, and he

5

sensed the power within those words flow from his tongue to his veins to the hand holding the sword. The power spread to the surrounding air, summoning forth the wind. Air whipped around the leaf-shaped blade, then with a thrust of the sword, Maugis willed the wind forward. It struck the lanky man with the force of a gale, lifting him off his feet until Maugis turned the sword's tip toward the ground and the violent wind slammed the man hard onto the cobblestones.

Sprawled in a puddle of sewage, the lanky man let out a long, pain-filled groan. The wind had cleaned Maugis' blade of the burly man's blood, so he slid the sword into its sheath and picked his quarterstaff off the ground. He walked gingerly toward the lanky man, already feeling the weakness creeping into his limbs. As Orionde had taught him years ago, invoking the power came with a price. But this was no time to worry about exhaustion. He had to know who sent these men.

He crouched beside the lanky man. "Who is the Blackbird?"

"We've never seen him," the man whimpered. "I swear. He only works through a messenger. If we had known you were one of the twelve, we would have never taken the job."

The man was referring to the paladins, the twelve peers of King Charles of Francia, and Maugis was chief among them. It was no wonder that their employer had not told these two about Maugis' identity. Few men in Paris would trifle with one of the paladins, let alone one secretly trained in the arts of the ancient magi. "Who was the messenger?" Maugis demanded.

"It was a woman," the lanky man said, "but I never seen her. Grimoald was the one who met her. She paid him."

Maugis glanced back at the burly man laying dead in the alleyway and cursed under his breath. Of the two of these fools, he had killed the wrong one. Maugis was about to ask where Grimoald and this messenger met when he sensed a disturbance in the air. For a breath, it felt thick and pungent, like a breeze before a thunderstorm. But instead of a crack of thunder, he heard a subtle sound like a viper's hiss, followed by a faint sizzle in the air. Maugis had experienced this sensation before, and its implications sent a chill racing down his spine. For somewhere nearby, another type of summoning had just taken place. One born of necromancy and the dark arts that no man was ever meant to wield. Someone had discovered his mission and hired these two fools. And whoever it was may have just summoned something from the Otherworld, placing the whole mission in peril.

The time for interrogations was over. Maugis cast one last glance at the lanky man, before hammering his quarterstaff across the man's skull. Then he grabbed his book satchel and ran off toward the wharves with whatever strength he had left in his legs.

At the old Roman wharf, sloops, merchant ships, and fishing boats swayed in the gentle current of the Seine. The docks were devoid of people at this hour save for a hulking man with an ample gray beard waiting in front of a small ship with a furled sail. Although he was built like a bear, the sixty-year-old Archbishop of Reims could have passed for a grizzled dockworker in his old traveling cloak and simple brown tunic. The outfit was a far cry from the crimson vestments he often wore, befitting his high office.

"Turpin," Maugis called to the archbishop, "we must hurry! We've been found out."

Turpin furrowed his thick brow. "How can you be sure?"

"They'll be time to explain when we're on the river," Maugis said. "But if we don't leave now, I fear something bad is about to happen."

"How bad?"

"Like Verona bad."

Turpin's eyes widened. "That bad, eh? Then by God and good Saint Denis, get on board. Roland and Bradamante should be right behind you."

Maugis jumped into the ship and breathed a sigh of relief when he spotted Roland and Bradamante at the far end of the wharf. The mission would require all four of their skill sets, just as Orionde had foretold, and now their team was complete. Even more, in a few moments they would set off from Paris and their quest would be underway. Feeling the weight of this moment, Maugis made the sign of the cross and whispered a prayer for the mission's success.

For the fate of all of Christendom depended on it.

2

THE BREWING STORM

A haze of fog clung to the waters of the Seine as the small merchant vessel cast off from the Paris wharf. Maugis welcomed the damp mist because it would help conceal their departure. Even though someone in Paris had discovered their mission and maybe its purpose, they never could have learned his precise destination. Maugis had kept that secret even from the three companions he traveled with now. And anyone spying on them from the walls of Paris would not know which way their boat was going, either upriver or down, once it became lost in the murk.

The fog was a faint comfort, but it would have to do while Maugis set his mind on rowing. The boat, with a single mast and four oarports on each side, was built for a crew of eight, but they would have to suffice with only half that. Maugis could not risk the lives of any more of the King's paladins on this mission, and he had reasons to doubt that anyone other than his three companions could be trusted.

They rowed in silence for fear that voices carry over water, and Maugis believed it would not be safe to speak until they were well away from the city. Roland manned the bench in front of Maugis, pulling his oar with the strength of a seasoned warrior. Strong-jawed and handsome, the thirty-two-year-old chevalier was dressed like the rest of them in a plain woolen cloak, a tunic, and breeches. He had stowed his chainmail hauberk beneath the bench, along with a shield covered in dark leather and his longsword, Durendal, the most legendary weapon in the realm. Charles would be furious when he learned Maugis had absconded with the Lord Commander of the Breton March, but Maugis would deal with the King's anger if they made it back alive. The object of their quest was more important than anything he could imagine, and there was no warrior in Francia more skilled than Roland.

Beside Roland, Turpin rowed with a steady rhythm. Despite his years, the gray-bearded cleric was stronger than most men half his age. But it was not his brawn that Maugis wanted on this mission. Rather, Maugis needed the archbishop's keen mind and his vast knowledge of things both spiritual and supernatural. If their hidden enemy had the power to summon something from the Otherworld, Turpin's talents may be more valuable now than ever before.

Roland's cousin, Bradamante, worked the oar next to Maugis. She was the rarest of things in Francia: a woman, as beautiful as any maiden, yet skilled in the warrior's ways with a prowess in battle that could match that of the most seasoned chevalier. Maugis could only surmise that these talents ran thick in the bloodline of Roland's family. And while Maugis had wanted to spare her from this mission, Orionde had insisted that Bradamante would be vital to its success. "You will need a woman's intuition," Orionde had said, "and a companion with a fortitude of mind far stronger than you men possess. She must go."

After rowing for a time, Turpin turned toward Maugis. "We're far enough away. Tell us what went on back there."

"In one of the alleyways between the palace and the docks, I happened upon two fellows who had a keen interest in slitting my throat. At first, I thought they were common thieves, but then I learned they had been hired. They knew I'd be going to the wharf, and whoever paid them wanted my book."

Bradamante ran a hand over her auburn hair tied back in a ponytail. "Someone paid them to attack you, and you think they knew of the mission? How's that possible?"

"I wish I knew," Maugis said. "I've not told more than the three of you. But nonetheless, Orionde feared the King may have a spy in his court."

"And how would she know?" Roland asked. "It's not as if she's ever been near the King's court. Besides, I trust our peers."

Turpin snickered. "I'd no more trust Ganelon than I would a silver fox near my henhouse."

"But you think he'd be caught up in this affair?" Roland shook his head. "Ganelon's a creature of court. He may use his cunning to win Charles's favor at times, but this business of ours is not some game to win a seat next to the throne. It's the stuff of angels and demons, and Ganelon's not the type of man to obsess about such things."

"Whoever it is goes by an alias," Maugis said. "The thieves who attacked me called their employer the Blackbird. But there's more. When I dispatched the men, I sensed something. A feeling I've experienced before when someone has opened a gateway to the Otherworld and drawn forth something from its depths. It's the same sensation I felt in Verona."

"Are you certain?" Bradamante asked with a hint of alarm.

Maugis gave a sigh. "I wish I wasn't."

"Well, that's a cheery thought for this fine morn," Roland quipped.

"We all survived Verona," Turpin said, "and we're wiser for it. But it's troubling to believe there's been a sorcerer hiding in the court, and right under our noses."

"Orionde has long cautioned that the enemy's servants are always watching," Maugis told them. "Some lurk in the shadows, while others hide in plain sight. She warned they would come for us if they suspected we knew where the device was hidden. All we can do now is remain vigilant."

Turpin answered with a solemn nod. "If Orionde is what you say she is, I won't doubt her words."

"Ah yes, in Orionde we trust!" Roland craned his neck toward Maugis. "One day, I would very much like to meet this mysterious woman who tells us what to do and delights in tangling up your mind with riddles."

"If we return with the device," Maugis replied, "I'm certain you'll get your chance."

Bradamante flashed a mischievous grin. "Roland just wants to see if she's as beautiful as you claim. Isn't that right, cousin?"

"Hardly," Roland said with a trace of blush in his cheeks. "Who wouldn't want to meet the woman who pulls Maugis' strings like a puppeteer and sends us off on a quest to find some weapon that can prevent the End of Days? She seems fascinating."

"Yes, I'm sure that's it." Bradamante rolled her eyes. "Worry not, Maugis, I'll keep watch. And my mind's not nearly as distracted as my cousin's."

Maugis smiled. "I could not ask for more." And it was true. He trusted these three more than anyone in his life, and, besides King Charles, they were the only ones who believed the truth about Maugis and the power he could wield. It was among the few reasons he could entrust them on this mission and talk so freely about the arcane matters surrounding it.

To speak so candidly to anyone else, particularly within earshot of one of the clergy, would be to risk condemnation, and even a far worse fate. Almost every cleric in Christendom, from the country parish priests to the Holy Father in Rome, believed that all things men called magic or witchcraft came from demons. And anyone who dabbled in those arts should burn at the stake. The priests and bishops presided over these grisly executions, believing they were carrying out God's will, and who could blame them. After all, the Book of Exodus commands that no sorcerer shall be permitted to live.

Turpin, however, was the only cleric Maugis had ever known to open his mind to the existence of a more complicated reality. For it was true that some arts, such as the conjuring he sensed in the alleyway, were evil, born of unholy practices that date back to a dark and secret history only hinted of in Scripture. But there were other arts, such as those practiced by the magi of Persia, whose origins were even more ancient, and far purer. These secrets belonged to the immortal beings men called angels and were entrusted by some of their kind to mortals whom they deemed worthy of mastering such mysteries. As centuries passed, this secret truth became obscured within pagan myths, and most priests would agree that all things pagan are heresy, and all heretics must burn. Fortunately for Maugis, his three friends held a more enlightened view of things.

Maugis' mind settled on more peaceful thoughts by midmorning when the fog burned off the water, and the gray skies gave way to sunshine and a swath of blue. The breeze picked up, so they unfurled the sail and let the newfound wind do much of the work.

The Seine meandered through the dense forests and green meadows of Northern Francia. Occasionally, a small village or farmstead appeared around the bend of the riverbank, along with a priory or two, or a parish church. Near these settlements, fishing boats worked the river, their crews using nets to catch salmon, eels, and redeye. These vessels looked as if they belonged to the local villagers, and none of them gave Maugis pause. No boats or ships had followed them from Paris. Of that, he was certain.

After midday, they lunched on a meal of bread and hard cheese and shared a skin of ale. As they were passing the ale, a shadow fell over them. Maugis glanced up. A cluster of angry gray clouds had emerged to the west, blocking half the sun.

"That storm came up suddenly for this time of year," Turpin said. "Should we take shelter?"

Roland waved him off. "The clouds are leagues to the west. We'll be fine."

"Roland's right," Maugis said, "but let's keep an eye on it. After another league on the river, we can look for a place to spend the night."

Within the hour, the temperature dropped, and the breeze grew quiet. Soon, the sail hung flaccidly from the yard, forcing Maugis and his companions to return to rowing. "Those clouds are coming in fast," Bradamante observed.

Maugis glanced over his shoulder. The storm-clouds loomed over the treetops, and he watched as they moved over the river to the south, only to waft eastward, as if the storm was following the curvature of the waterway.

"Have you ever seen a storm move like that?" Turpin asked, his face as gray as his beard.

"Never," Roland replied.

The storm had taken on a deep, charcoal hue. The head of the clouds billowed in their direction like a titanic serpent twisting its body toward them, as if it had picked up their scent with its flicking forked tongue.

"I swear they're following us," Bradamante said, staring wide-eyed.

A chill washed over Maugis' skin. Given the sensation he had felt in the alleyway, he had to know if she was right. He set his thoughts on the ring on his left hand. The square crystal in its center polished as smooth as glass, appeared opaque, but it would not stay that way for long. Clearing his mind, he drew in a breath and whispered a word: *Eoh*. It was the first of the arcane words that Orionde had taught him, and with the whisper of his breath, it infused the gemstone with the light of his soul. The light began as a bright spark within the crystal, then settled into a white glow that formed a nimbus around Maugis' hand. *Let the truth be revealed through the light.*

Maugis peered through the glow of his soul light, and what he witnessed made his blood run cold.

"What do you see?" Turpin asked.

"That's no storm," Maugis said grimly. "That thing summoned in Paris—it's found us."

3

HALLOWED GROUND

Through the glow of his soul light, Maugis gazed upon a nightmare. Surrounded by vapors at the head of the storm, and borne aloft by its winds, flew a translucent creature, gigantic in size and vaguely human in shape. What he could make of its face appeared twisted with a feral rage around eyes smoldering like embers while blueish flames spilled off its ghostly form, burning like a Beltane fire.

"What is it?" Turpin asked.

"One of the *Mazikeen*," Maugis said, recalling the term Orionde once used for such things. "In Hebrew, it means 'bringer of storms.' They're a type of demon, and this one looks as mad as hell."

Roland reached under his bench and ripped Durendal from its scabbard. Scrollwork gleamed down the polished blade.

"That won't be any use against this demon," Maugis warned.

Roland swore under his breath. "Then how do we stop it?"

"We can't right now," Maugis said hastily. "All we can hope to do is outrun it."

"But it's moving too fast." Bradamante could not take her eyes off the black storm billowing toward them like a thunderhead.

Maugis knew they could not outpace the demon with their oars, but there was another way. He reached under the oar bench where he had stowed his hauberk and other belongings until he found his leaf-bladed sword. After asking his friends to move to the stern or the prow, he stood up in the hull and began waving the blade in a circular motion. As he recited the verse, the familiar surge of power caused the air to thrum, and once again, the wind obeyed his command. It whipped around the blade until Maugis directed it straight at the sail. The sailcloth bowed, and the rigging snapped taut, and within a breath, the wind was propelling the vessel forward.

"I'll steer the boat," Bradamante called from the stern. "You get us out of here."

Maugis gave her a nod, trying to keep his concentration on the wind. A momentary lapse in focus could doom his effort.

As the vessel gained speed, water sprayed over the gunwales, but the storm was keeping pace—even gaining.

"We must find hallowed ground," Turpin said with grim determination.

"What will that do?" Roland asked.

Turpin glared at him. "Think man! An evil spirit cannot cross onto hallowed ground."

"I'm just asking," Roland insisted. "This is my first *Mazikeen*."

Maugis agreed with Turpin. "It might keep it at bay, and it would buy us much needed time."

"Maugis, can you go any faster?" Bradamante asked with an edge of concern in her voice.

He glanced back. The storm was nearly above them, and he could sense its energy drawing heat from the air. "This is as fast as I can go. Look for shelter!"

"Over there!" Roland pointed to an eastward bend in the river where a stone tower rose above rolling green hills. A cross-shaped finial topped its steeple.

"It's an abbey," Turpin said. "Hallowed ground!"

Gripping the tiller, Bradamante guided the vessel around the riverbend while Maugis focused all his energy on the wind. Ahead, he spied a dilapidated pier on the east bank near a road that led to the abbey. A curtain wall protected the abbey's structures, some made of wood, while the church and the buildings surrounding the cloister were built of stone with slate roofs, a hallmark of the monasteries built by the old Merovingian kings.

"Head for that pier!" Maugis called to Bradamante over the roar of the wind whipping off the storm. The storm-winds battered against him with the force of a gale, overwhelming the wind he had summoned. He struggled to regain control when a violent gust threw him forward. He hit the mast hard as the howling gale ripped the sail from its yard. The storm-winds sent the ship careening toward the pier. Maugis wrapped his arms around the mast right before the vessel smashed through a rickety fishing boat and slammed into the moorings. Planks snapped, and, with a cry, Roland and Turpin went flying from the boat. Maugis grabbed hold of Bradamante with his left hand, keeping her in the vessel, but water was pouring in through a gash in the hull and pooling around his ankles.

The storm loomed over the broken pier like the wrath of some angry god. "Run for the abbey!" Maugis yelled as he grabbed his satchel and staff from beneath the oar bench. Beside him, Bradamante tossed Durendal to Roland, retrieved her own blade, and jumped onto the pier. Weakness crept into Maugis' limbs, the price of wielding the power, but he fought his exhaustion and leaped onto the riverbank. He landed on a muddied patch of grass while overhead came a crack like thunder followed by the hiss of rain. But instead of drenching water came a flurry of hail.

Hailstones battered Maugis' shoulders and back, pain searing with each strike. He tried to protect his head with his arm and staff, but a hailstone the size of a silver coin grazed his cheek, so cold it burned. He knew they wouldn't last long in this.

Roland and Turpin shielded their heads from the raging hailstorm as they sprinted toward the abbey's gatehouse. "Open the gate!" the archbishop cried.

The hailstorm roared around them, littering the ground with frozen pellets. Bradamante slipped and tumbled to the hail-strewn earth. Maugis lunged to help her to her feet. "Let's go," he urged. She nodded, though blood trickled down her forehead as the hailstones continued their assault.

Ahead of them, Roland and Turpin pounded on the abbey's gate when the hiss of hail ceased. A blast of air whooshed behind Maugis, almost spinning him around. Over the pier, the black cloud had diminished in size but was now swirling in violent circles, sucking up the surrounding air and forming a funnel-like shape.

Bradamante gasped. Maugis felt a surge of fear as the whirling tempest rushed forward, tearing up dirt and hail in its path. He grabbed Bradamante by the hand and ran with all that remained of his strength. Yet from the growing sound of the storm's roar, he knew it was moving faster than they were.

At the abbey, Roland hammered Durendal's pommel into the wooden gate. "In the name of the King, open the bloody door!"

The gate cracked open. Turpin reached his hands around the gate's edge and, with a shout, wrenched it wide open.

Thirty paces from the abbey, the wind drew Maugis and Bradamante toward the funnel. Maugis fought to move forward, his thighs burning as if he was trying to scale the side of a steep hill. Roland hurried toward them. He grabbed Bradamante by her left hand as Maugis clung to her right arm. Clenching his teeth, Roland pulled them toward the gate, but Maugis could feel the wind whipping at his cloak. He feared it was nearly upon them.

But then Turpin was there. The archbishop wrapped a thick arm around Roland's chest and tugged with all his might. In the tug of war between wind and man, Turpin's strength made the difference as he hauled the three of them through the gateway and into the abbey's courtyard. A monk slammed the gate shut behind them as a wail shrieked from the tempest—a sound of sheer rage. As quickly as the funnel had formed, it dissipated before reaching the abbey's gate. Above the curtain wall, the remnants of the funnel-cloud billowed skyward, retreating toward the river until they reformed into an angry, storm-like shape, casting a dark shadow over the abbey.

Turpin embraced his three friends. "Thank God and good Saint Denis. We're on hallowed ground."

4

THE BOOK OF MAUGIS
D'AYGREMONT

The monk who slammed the gate shut stared slack-jawed at Maugis and his companions. He was no older than eighteen, if Maugis had to guess, but stood a hair shy of Turpin's height, with a blunt nose and a face marred by pox scars. A black Benedictine habit engulfed his muscular frame, though judging from the dim look in his eyes, Maugis suspected the man had not taken his solemn vows. More likely, he was illiterate and common-born, one of the lay brothers hired to serve as the abbey's gatekeeper.

"What was that?" the gatekeeper asked over the bleating of a pen full of fearful sheep and the cackling of chickens, who stood clustered together near the abbey's stables as if they had just encountered a fox.

"There's an evil in that wind," Turpin told him. "But fear not, it cannot cross onto the hallowed ground of this place. That's why you saw it retreat before it reached the gate."

The gatekeeper's face turned ashen, and he seemed at a loss for words.

Roland looked at Maugis. "You're bleeding."

Maugis touched his cheek. His fingertips were with slick with blood. "Thanks." He reached into a belt pouch and found a vial of his elixir. An illness since childhood had thinned his blood, but the mixture brewed from mulled blackberry leaf, mullein, and bee pollen would help it clot. He uncorked the vial with his thumb and swallowed the dose. The bitter liquid burned his throat, though it was preferable to bleeding to death from a minor flesh wound.

Bradamante wiped a splash of blood off her forehead. "What do we do now?"

"We find a way to stop it," Maugis replied. "Orionde taught me how to deal with these spirits, so I hope the solution's right in here." He patted the side of his satchel. "I just need a quiet place to study it."

"Whatever was that sound?" a voice demanded from the far end of the courtyard.

Maugis craned his neck to see a squat, older monk emerge from the abbey's church. His reddening face was as wrinkled as a dried apricot, and milk-white hair surrounded his tonsure. A half-score of black-robed monks scurried behind the man, who must have been the abbot, given the gilded crucifix dangling at his chest.

"T'was a tempest, Lord Abbot," the gatekeeper admitted. "It came out of nowhere."

The abbot made a pinched expression as he strode past a rickety wheelbarrow and an old stone well with a winch and a wood-shingle roof in the center of the courtyard. "A tempest?" He peered at the black cloud that had settled over the Seine. "I see no damage. And who are these men?" The abbot's eyes widened. "And that ... woman?"

Bradamante curled her lips at the abbot's condescending tone. Meanwhile, Turpin glanced at Maugis.

As much as Maugis had hoped to keep this mission secret, whoever summoned that demon already knew what he and his friends were up to. And right now, they needed aid more than secrecy. "Go ahead and tell him," Maugis said. "We'll need his help if we have any hope of leaving here."

Turpin answered with a nod, then turned to the abbot, whose head barely reached Turpin's chest. "I am Archbishop Turpin of Reims. I travel with Count Roland, Lord Commander of the Breton March, his cousin, the Lady Bradamante, and Count Maugis d'Aygremont, chief counselor to his highness, King Charles."

The abbot's expression grew more pinched. "You are not dressed like lords? For all I know, you're lying and seek to rob us."

Roland gave a long sigh. With a scrape of steel, he unsheathed Durendal. At the sight of the broadsword, the abbot flinched; behind him, a gasp rose from the gaggle of monks. Scrollwork gleamed down the sword's blade, though the abbot's gaze settled on its pommel and cross-guard plated in gleaming gold. "This is Durendal," Roland announced in a commanding tone, "forged of the same steel as Joyeuse, the blade of King Charles. It is the sword that slew a hundred men at the Battle of Verona. Only the king's champion wields such a blade. So, tell me, Lord Abbot, do you still doubt who we are?"

A flush crept across the abbot's cheeks. "Are you here on the King's business?"

"The nature of our business is no business of yours," Maugis said. "We were on the river. When the storm fell upon us, we sought refuge here."

The abbot's gaze darted between the double-edged broadsword and Turpin. The abbot swallowed hard. "Who am I to deny refuge to the King's men?" he replied humbly. "May I offer you accommodations in our guesthouse tonight?"

"That would be good of you," Maugis said. "But first, we must visit your scriptorium."

The abbot cocked his head. "Whatever for?"

"The King's business," Maugis lied.

"I suppose it's possible," the abbot said. "Our scriptorium is of modest size, but it's free right now."

Maugis and his companions followed the abbot into the cloister. Halfway around the cloister, the abbot opened the door to the scriptorium. Slanted desks cluttered with rolls of parchment, inkpots, and feathered quills filled the cramped chamber. A row of narrow windows covered in oiled sheepskin let ample light in for the scribes who used this space to copy and illuminate manuscripts. But right now, the scriptorium was empty.

"This will suffice," Maugis said before bidding the abbot farewell. As soon as he was gone, Maugis retrieved the leather-bound tome from his satchel. A cross-shaped symbol with a looped head was pressed into the black leather book cover. Turpin would recognize the symbol as an Egyptian Ankh, though Maugis knew the symbol's origins were much older than the ancient pharaohs. He set the book on one of the slanted desks and unlatched the iron clasps that held the tome closed. As he opened the book, the scent of vellum filled the air.

"Something in that book is supposed to help us defeat that demon?" Roland asked skeptically.

"Every secret Orionde ever taught me is written in this tome," Maugis said, "and she knew how to deal with demons." He sat down at the bench behind the desk and began leafing through pages. Some were filled with scrawling text, and others with shapes—triangles and circles adorned with astrological symbols, elaborately drawn letters, or Arabic numerals. Several pages had both words and drawings, while many revealed nothing but stained vellum, without even a splotch of ink.

"Half the pages are blank?" Roland observed.

Maugis smiled. "They're not, actually. You just need to read them in the proper light." He drew in a deep breath, clearing his thoughts. Then he whispered into the gemstone set into his ring. *Eoh* ... White light flared within the gem, and in its glow, a series of words began scrolling down the blank pages. Diagrams emerged too, decorated with symbols, several of which vaguely resembled letters, though others were more exotic and glyph-like, all fragments of a language more ancient than mankind.

"It never ceases to amaze," Turpin said, watching the words and symbols materialize on the pages.

Roland's eyes widened with awe. "Someday, you must tell me how you met this extraordinary woman who taught you this magic."

Maugis glanced up. "Someday, I will. But first, let's deal with this demon."

His gaze crawled down the vellum page until he found the words he was looking for above a drawing of a protective circle with a seven-pointed star in its center. A heading topped the page: *On the warding and binding of demons.* He studied Orionde's instructions, reading them several times until the task that lay ahead became firmly rooted in his mind. He looked up to his friends, huddled in the scriptorium. "We'll need a vessel," he announced, "made of precious metal."

"You mean to trap it?" Turpin asked.

"Yes," Maugis said with a nod.

Bradamante shook her head. "Where will we find something to trap a demon?"

Turpin grinned. "In the church, of course."

"A reliquary," Roland replied with a clap of his hands. "I'll be right back." He opened the door and darted into the cloister.

"The abbot will not like that," Bradamante opined.

Maugis shrugged. "He won't enjoy being held captive in this abbey either. Yet that's what will happen so long as that storm's outside." He kept reading through the next steps in the binding process, then frowned. "There's still one problem."

"What?" Turpin asked.

"For this to work, we must find out its name."

Turpin furrowed his brow. "How do you propose we do that?"

"I'm still working on it," Maugis admitted. It was the one problem Orionde's instructions did not solve. She had suggested the task could be accomplished through trickery or torture, but a demon's true name was a precious possession, and the evil spirit was not wont to make it known. As he searched for a better answer in the arcane text, a cry rang from the cloister.

"Unhand that!"

The door flew open, and Roland emerged holding a bronze casket the size of a breadbasket. The abbot, his face red, stormed after Roland, while a troupe of monks trailed behind them.

"That casket contains the toes of Saint Julian!" the abbot exclaimed with indignation. "It's one of our most sacred relics!"

Maugis let the light fade from the gemstone in his ring, and as it disappeared, so did the words on the page. He stood up from the bench. "I know of a reliquary in Paris that holds the saint's toes," he told the abbot. "All ten of them. How many toes did poor Saint Julian have?"

The abbot blanched. "You dare challenge the authenticity of our most precious relic!"

"Will it do?" Roland asked Maugis, ignoring the abbot. The reliquary was trimmed in brass, and images of the apostles adorned its bronze sides. A brass latch held its hinged lid shut.

"It's perfect," Maugis said.

The abbot gasped as Roland tossed the casket to Maugis. Something bone-like clattered inside.

"Give it back!" the abbot demanded.

"Listen," Turpin interjected, standing to his full, imposing height. "There's something wicked in that storm. An unholy spirit that commands its fury. Yet with that casket, we might be able to stop it."

The abbot's palms flew to his head. "Have you all gone mad?"

As if to answer the question, a roar of wind blared from outside the abbey. Cries filled with terror followed the roar, emanating from the courtyard. Maugis felt a pang of dread in his stomach. "You're about to learn the truth," he growled at the abbot as he cradled the casket beneath his left arm and rushed into the cloister.

5

THE FACE OF FEAR

Maugis found the courtyard in complete pandemonium. Terrified sheep bleated fearfully in their pen and chickens scurried about frantically. A dozen panicked monks stared at the gatehouse. Some uttered prayers while others clutched their chests, gaping at what was happening.

The abbey's open gate swung back and forth on its hinges, and before it, at the courtyard's threshold, the gatekeeper held up a wild-haired villager, as if he had rescued the man from the storm. But beyond the curtain wall, the storm was nowhere to be seen. A platinum-gray sky had taken its place while a hissing wind soughed through the nearby trees.

Maugis' thoughts whirled in his mind. He grabbed the shoulder of the nearest monk. "What just happened?"

"Fisherman Faronis got caught in the storm," the monk replied, his eyes wide. "The cloud descended upon him, roaring like the devil. We feared it would swallow him whole. But Lay Brother Hugo opened the gate and ran out and saved him!"

Turpin hurried to Maugis' side. "I don't like the looks of this," the archbishop said.

"Neither do I," Maugis replied.

A portly monk slammed the abbey's gate shut. Meanwhile, the gatekeeper hunched over the weather-beaten fisherman, who had dropped to a knee and was retching on the ground. A breath later, the abbot stormed past Roland and Bradamante with his entourage of monks in tow. The abbot's face had turned a new shade of red. "What in the name of Saint Denis is going on!"

A pallid-faced monk began to explain. "Fisherman Faronis got caught in the storm!"

The abbot's eyes narrowed. "The storm—where did it go?"

"It blew away, as soon as Lay Brother Hugo reached Faronis," the monk said.

That new bit of information made Maugis' skin chill. His gaze darted to the fisherman, whose face was twisting into a malevolent sneer. In a breath, the fisherman lunged toward the portly monk who had closed the gate. Grabbing him by his habit, the fisherman pressed a flaying knife to the monk's neck. As a gasp rose from the monks gathered in the courtyard, the flesh around the fisherman's eyes darkened, and he began to speak. His voice was harsh and deep with the hint of something unnatural behind it. "Where is the book of Maugis d'Aygremont?"

Maugis tried to steel his nerves as he stared into the possessed man's eyes. "Is that why you're here?" He could not explain how the demon could stand on the abbey's hallowed ground, but this was no time for theorizing.

"The secrets in that book were not meant for you," the fisherman said coldly. "Now, tell me where the book is, or I will kill this monk and everyone in this abbey."

The abbot stepped forward with a horrified look on his face. "His book is in the scriptorium. Take it and leave us be!"

The fisherman's grin widened. He tossed the portly monk aside as if he weighed no more than a child. The monk cried out, his arms windmilling as he thudded into the curtain wall. Then the fisherman raised his arms into the air and uttered a verse in a strange, foreign tongue. Maugis' breath caught in his throat as he recognized the final word. *"Come!"*

From atop the church came a hideous shriek. A dark cloud of wings and fur burst from the archways supporting the bellower. A cloud of bats flew helter-skelter into the courtyard. At the same time, a high-pitched squeal erupted from the well in the courtyard's center before a horde of rats spilled over its rim, their claws chattering on the stone.

The abbot and his monks cried out in terror as the bats dove recklessly toward them and the chittering rats overwhelmed the grounds. Maugis swatted away a trio of bats flittering toward him, though a fourth landed on his cloak, tearing at it with its teeth. Rats kept pouring from the well, and he kicked one away, only to have another crawl up his boot and gnaw at his calf.

"So much for hallowed ground," Roland said under his breath as he tore Durendal from its sheath and cleaved at a swarm of bats diving for his face. Bradamante swung at them too, slicing at the flying rodents, who swerved to avoid the strike. Their swords proved to be poor weapons against the rats as well, who sprung from the ground, attacking the warriors as if they were a carrion feast.

Amidst the chaos, the possessed man charged toward the cloister. He rumbled through a pair of screaming monks, knocking them to the ground where they were overcome by the swelling sea of rats.

"Stop him!" Maugis cried before whacking away a squealing bat with the casket held tight in his left arm.

Ripping rats off his tunic, Turpin heeded Maugis' call. An old wheelbarrow stood between the archbishop and the possessed man. With a roar, Turpin grabbed the wheelbarrow and smashed it into the charging fisherman. Wood splintered in every direction as the blow threw the fisherman hard onto the ground. Before he could spring to his feet, Turpin drove a knee into the man's chest, followed by a fist to the man's face. "In the name of the Father!" Turpin yelled, landing another blow. "And the Son!" His fist pounded the man a third time. "And the Holy Spirit!"

Turpin continued his beating, this time in the name of each of the apostles, ignoring the rats scratching at his back and shoulders. "For Saint James, and Saint Thomas, and Saint John!" With each of Turpin's blows, the fisherman looked more dazed, and Maugis knew this was his chance. He pulled a rat off his thigh and drew in a breath before whispering *"Eoh"* into the gemstone in his ring. As his soul light blazed within the gem, he thrust it into the possessed man's face. In the light's glow, Maugis once again glimpsed the demon's visage. Vaguely human and contorted with rage. Its eyes burned like hot coals, and jagged fangs filled its mouth.

Maugis gathered his thoughts, forming a wall around his mind, for he could feel the demon's own thoughts boring into his skull. With a grimace, Maugis willed the light forward with all his might. White light blasted into the demon's eyes, as it howled in pain. "Tell me your name, dammit!" Maugis demanded.

The light seared the flesh around the man's eyes. In its glow, the demonic visage shuddered in agony. *"FEAR!"* the demon roared. With a surge of inhuman strength, he threw Maugis and Turpin off him. The possessed man leaped to his feet and staggered into the cloister.

Maugis shook his head in frustration. Fear was not a name. Even more, the possessed man was escaping.

Turpin pulled Maugis to his feet. An idea gleamed in the archbishop's eyes. "Maugis," he said, "think of the ancient Greeks!"

Turpin's words struck Maugis like a thunderbolt. Perhaps the demon *had* revealed his name! He grabbed hold of the casket and darted into the cloister. At the far end, the scriptorium's door hung open. Recalling each word of Orionde's instructions, he ducked inside.

Within the chamber, the possessed man clutched Maugis' book to his chest. "You're too late," he rasped.

"And you're wrong." Maugis began speaking each word of the verse memorized from his book. With each syllable, the surrounding air thrummed. The possessed man stood transfixed only to gasp in horror when Maugis cracked the casket's lid and uttered the demon's true name: *"Phobos!"*

A sudden blast of wind whipped through the scriptorium. A shimmer of blue flames surrounded the possessed man, who let out a horrid cry. Blue fire streaked from his body into the casket, and in its light, Maugis witnessed the tormented image of the demon streaming helplessly into its new prison. As he closed the casket's lid, he heard the rattle of bones and the hint of a tortured wail.

Maugis' mouth stretched into a grin. Maybe those were Saint Julian's toes after all?

6

REFLECTIONS

I nside the warm confines of the abbey's refectory, Maugis swallowed a spoonful of pease porridge and chased it with a hunk of bread and a gulp of wine. His battle with the demon had left him feeling famished, and as bland as the abbey's food was, he welcomed it like a Midsummer's feast.

As soon as Maugis had imprisoned the demon, the horde of rats and bats it had summoned scattered like frightened field mice. Though bitten and bruised, the abbot and his fellow monks had survived the attack. And while a dozen of the abbey's brethren had been sent to the infirmary, the abbot was left mostly unscathed. Ever since then, he had been falling over himself to express his gratitude toward Maugis and his companions. First, he had a group of monks retrieve the rest of the companions' waterlogged belongings from their wrecked ship. The large pile of chain mail, shields, weapons, and sacks were laid near the hearth to dry, though Maugis knew they'd need to polish the armor and weapons in the morning to prevent them from rusting. Next, the abbot ordered his cellarer to bring whatever food they had prepared to the refectory in honor of the abbey's noble guests, only to apologize when he discovered it was nothing more than a pot of pease porridge, four loaves of bread, and a block of mold-ridden cheese. But he insisted his abbey's cellar had barrels of wine from Brittany, and Turpin implored him to bring up as many carafes as they could drink.

The monks did not delay in bringing the wine, and Turpin was the first to pour himself a cup. "To God and good Saint Denis," he said, raising a toast.

"Amen," Bradamante replied.

At the far end of the table, the casket rattled. The startled abbot jumped back a step while the monks who had brought the wine scurried from the room.

"Fear not," Maugis assured him. "It can't escape. I've made certain of that."

The abbot made the sign of the cross. "Forgive me lords for ever doubting you. I fear I was unaware the King's counselor was such a formidable exorcist."

"This wine is all the amends you need give," Turpin said, having already drained his first cup.

After the abbot had left them alone to their meal, Bradamante posed a question. "How did you figure out the demon's name?"

"I didn't," Maugis replied, before swallowing a mouthful of wine. "Turpin did."

"And?" Roland gestured at Turpin.

The old cleric flashed a clever grin between his wine-flushed cheeks. "It was a theory based on mythology—and everything Maugis had ever taught me about it, of course."

"Do tell," Bradamante said. Even with her hair a tangled mess from the confrontation in the courtyard, Maugis thought she looked beautiful in the light from the nearby hearth.

Turpin poured himself another cup of wine before offering his explanation. "In one of our many discussions about the supernatural over the years, Maugis convinced me that evil spirits were the condemned souls of the Nephilim."

"The what?" Roland asked.

"The Nephilim," Turpin repeated, "the unholy offspring of angels and men. They're written of in the sixth chapter of Genesis, before the account of the Great Flood. In the age where the sons of God—angels who came to Earth in defiance of the Holy Father—took wives of the daughters of men. In Hebrew, the word 'Nephilim' means 'the fallen.' But it also translates into the word 'giants.' Maugis theorized that these immense beings were once the gods and demigods of mythology."

Bradamante cocked her head. "So this demon was once a god?"

"Mythically speaking," Maugis replied.

"Right," Turpin continued. "No one has a more legendary mythology than the ancient Greeks. So when Maugis got the demon to say its name was 'Fear,' let's just say I had a hunch."

The archbishop took a gulp of wine. "You see, in Greek mythology the personification of fear is named Phobos. He's one of the twin sons of Ares, the god of war. Whenever Ares rode into battle, he took Phobos and his brother, Deimos, with him. Fear and Terror were their names, so when I heard the demon call itself 'Fear,' I suspected he might have been Phobos in another life. It turns out I was right—though it's a good thing Maugis here remembered his mythology."

"I had a relentless teacher," Maugis admitted.

Bradamante raised an eyebrow. "Orionde?"

"Mythology was one of her favorite subjects," Maugis explained.

"Ah," Roland said, "more talk of this mysterious woman. *Orionde le Fae*. Someday, I must know how you met this enchantress."

Bradamante shrugged. "Why not tell us now?"

"You truly want to know?" Maugis asked with a sigh.

Roland gave an eager nod. "What else are we going to do tonight?"

"If I must," Maugis said. "Though like every story, I suppose it's best to start at the beginning..."

II

MAUGIS' TALE

7

THE HUNT

I t all happened eleven years ago, but it really started well before then. You see, the story of how I met Orionde is a Faerie tale of sorts.

When I was a young boy, my grandmother lived with us at Aygremont, and she would tell me and my brother stories to warn us about the Fae. Faerie women, she said, would lure men into the woods and lead them to their haunted barrows, and the men would never be seen again. Other times the Fae would seduce their victims, drawing out a man's spirit with a fatal kiss, leaving their bodies but wasted husks amid the leafy duff. Grandmother passed away before my ninth birthday, and by the time I reached manhood, I had never seen one of the Fae. I began to wonder if her warnings were just stories adults told to scare unruly children. Yet in my nineteenth year, I saw one of the Fae in the flesh. It was in the autumn of 766, on the day of my father's hunt. The day that rent the House of Aygremont in two.

I was riding in the rear of the hunting party as it traipsed through my father's woods. I always rode in the back. You see, I had no love for the sport. I was among the rare breed of boy who preferred the touch of a book to the string of a bow, much to my father's dismay. Books, I found, were gateways to truths about the world, the kind that isn't self-evident to most men. As a boy, I was always fascinated by those truths. I still am. Back then, I thought anyone could go hunting, and what truths came from that?

Hunting with my father, however, was a family duty, and a miserable one too. Even if I wanted to, there was no need to ride near the front. For if the greyhounds found the royal stag they searched for, they would never grant me the privilege of killing it. That honor always went to my father or my brother, Vivian. Although we were twins, Vivian was the strong one to come from my mother's womb. His name came from the word *"vivus,"* which meant "alive." I, on the other hand, was born pale and sickly. The midwife said I was *"mal gist,"* lying badly, and that's why my father gave me the name Maugis. A cruel jest. But then again, my father was a cruel man.

My father, Count Bevis, rode at the head of the party astride his black charger. I still remember his wolf-fur cloak draped over his shoulders and his ivory hunting horn hanging at his side. My father was a man ruled by his passions. A passion for the hunt, a passion for ale, and a passion for women. So much so I overheard men in the castle saying that all Bevis ever thought with were his stomach and his loins.

My brother, Vivian, was no better, but he was far more cunning. With his long, dark hair tied behind his neck, he rode near Odulf, our father's huntsman. The grizzled huntsman traveled on foot, commanding his pack of greyhounds with the snap of his fingers and a sharp whistle. They nicknamed Odulf the "Lion" because of the cowl he wore made of the face and pelt of a mountain lion, the rarest of beasts in Francia and the huntsman's finest prize. The Lion was fiercely loyal to my father, and my father had rewarded him handsomely for that. Not only in silver but also by raising the ill-mannered man's station in life to that of a chevalier.

Behind the Lion, rode seven of Father's vassals. All were minor lords of the lands surrounding Aygremont who enjoyed hunting and drinking almost as much as my father. The lords trotted their steeds cautiously through the woods, searching for our quarry: a royal stag, rumored to be the most majestic beast in my father's forest. Men claimed it had six tines on each antler, and more than once during our pre-hunt meal, my father had boasted of mounting its head above the hearth. But since the hunt began, the greyhounds had not picked up the stag's scent, though earlier that morning the Lion had spotted its tracks through the carpet of autumn leaves. As midday neared, the only sound was the clomp of our horses' hooves over the forest duff and the hiss of a breeze that sent russet leaves wafting from the boughs.

"God's bones, Odulf," my father complained. "Do we need to put down these dogs and get some new ones? Why can't they find the bloody beast?"

"Patience, m'lord," the Lion said. "They'll sniff the stag out."

"I warned you, Father," Vivian added. "There have been whispers of poachers among the common folk."

My father scowled. "If someone's poached this hart, I'll burn him alive. His whole family too. Some men need hard lessons."

And some just need food for their families, I thought. Though I would never speak such thoughts aloud for fear of my father's fist. Even the lords who served my father were forbidden from hunting the red deer or wild boar outside his presence. While the lords could hunt hares or foxes, the only creatures the common folk were allowed to take from the woods were squirrels and badgers. It was no wonder it drove some men to poach, and it hardly warranted a death sentence in my view.

Father continued grousing about the poachers when the Lion held a finger to his lips. "Shh!" He pointed to a thicket of half-bare birch trees. Through the trunks I glimpsed the powerful hindquarters of a beast more massive than any buck. The greyhounds saw it too. The fur stood on their necks, but not one of them darted after the quarry.

Gripping his hunting lance, Father nodded at the Lion and nudged his horse forward. As the hunting party followed, the beast came more clearly into view. It was not a stag, but a horse. And on it, mounted bareback, was a woman so striking she stole my breath. Her limbs were slender, graceful, and mostly naked, covered only by the overhang of a gossamer shawl that clung to her breasts and waist. Her hair floated like spun silver on a breeze, its strands wisping across a face both beautiful and ageless. I glanced at my father, who seemed captivated by her stare.

In a breath, the woman turned away and bolted through the forest. A wake of fallen leaves stirred behind the rider as her mount danced deeper into the woods. "God's bones," father said, his voice thick with lust. He spurred his charger and chased after her like a hound that had caught the scent of a fox. Vivian glanced at the Lion, then followed after Father, a heartbeat before a cry rang from the woods. The cry of a beast—and one of a man.

"Father!" I yelled.

I rode toward the sound. When I reached Vivian, he was staring slack-jawed at Father and his charger. The stallion thrashed on the ground, half within a pit like one might dig to trap a feral hog. Beyond the pit, our father slumped at the base of a tree. His face was bloodied from impacting its trunk. But it was the sight of his neck that drew the bile to my throat. It was bent like no neck should, and at that moment I knew that my father, the fifteenth Count of Aygremont, lay dead.

Vivian dismounted and rushed to him. I leaped off my saddle and followed my brother, only to find Father's hunting lance lying on the ground. The gossamer shawl was wrapped around the lance's tip. It was the only sign remaining of the woman on the horse. I picked up the lance and reached out to touch the shawl. As my hand wrapped around it, the silky gauze dissolved within my grasp, running through my fingers like fine grains of sand. When it was gone, I glanced back at the freshly dug pit, and then to our father in Vivian's arms.

Grandmother used to warn of the Fae, and now I knew why. But that was the least of my worries. Far more concerning was the gleam in Vivian's eyes. For under the law, our father's domain would be split in two, one half to each brother. And as our kingdom's bloodstained history had proven, not all siblings were good with that.

8

THE FUNERAL

Our father's casket rested on a bier in the castle's chapel bathed in the light of beeswax candles. A shroud displaying the heraldry of the House of Aygremont—a golden leopard on a sable field—covered the casket. I stood to the left of the coffin while father's chaplain said the Mass. Vivian stood on the other side, beside the Lion and a slender woman who no doubt was another of Vivian's conquests. I could not see her face hidden within the deep cowl of her midnight cloak, save for a curl of raven hair against her cheek. Though like all of Vivian's lovers, I felt certain she was pretty.

Back then, I'm embarrassed to say, I had rarely known a woman's touch. The sickness that had stricken me as a child lingered into adulthood, leaving me pale, weak, and often short of breath. While the elixir the local apothecary brewed for me could relieve my condition, it should come as no surprise that maidens from Aygremont to Orleans favored my brother. When he caught me admiring the young woman by his side, he answered with a sharp gaze and a sly smile. I looked away and kept my head down until after the benediction. When the assembled vassals and members of the count's household said *"Deo gratias,"* I was among the first to leave the chapel.

JOSEPH FINLEY

After Mass, we put our father to rest in the crypt beneath the castle. Later that day, we held a feast in his honor. I sat at a trestle table on the opposite side of the great hall from Vivian. Our father's vassals and their wives crowded around my brother's table, obscuring but a glimpse of the young woman by his side. But the crowd of nobles sent a clear message about which of the two new lords of Aygremont would earn their fealty.

I ate in the shadow of an enormous aurochs head mounted on the wall. It was one of my father's many trophies displayed in the hall alongside the heads of stags, a black bear, and a pair of wild boars. I had barely touched my stew of mutton and broth when Odo sidled up on the bench beside me. Having hailed from my mother's home of Dordogne, Odo had served as our father's steward since before we were born. And ever since mother died of fever in the winter of 756, Odo had been like an uncle to me. He took a sip of his ale, its foam lingering on his short-cropped mustache and beard, both heavily laced with gray. "I don't like the looks of that, lad," he said, giving a subtle nod toward Vivian's table.

"Father's lords always favored Vivian," I replied.

"They've always been as daft as a flock of sheep too," Odo said with a wink.

"But Vivian's not."

"No." Odo pursed his lips. "Your brother's clever like a wolf. You know that, right?"

I nodded, poking a knife at my pork pie. "If Father could have chosen, he would have picked Vivian. Just like his fighting cocks, Father always preferred the strongest one. The most *ruthless* one."

"Lad, being ruthless is not what makes a good lord. A good lord protects those that need protecting. Like a sheepdog, not a wolf."

"Sheepdogs are strong. Me, not so much."

"But you're a man, not a dog. A man's true strength lies in the stuff between his ears." Odo tapped his finger to my forehead. "You think our King is the strongest of men? They call him Pepin the Short, for Christ's sake. His mind makes him strong. It's sharper than his sword."

"Our King commands an army of vassals," I said. "Ten thousand swordsmen and cavaliers are what makes him strong." I glanced at Vivian and the small army gathered around his table. Our father's lords were drinking and laughing, with the Lion foremost among them. The huntsman caught my gaze and gave me a hard smile. "I've lost my appetite," I told Odo and rose from the table.

"At least take an apple cake with you." Odo handed me one of the round, golden pastries. "The baker makes 'em with honey." The steward gave a faint smile as I took the cake and headed toward my chambers. Though as I left the hall, laughter echoed down the passageway, and I swore the Lion's bellows were the loudest—*and the cruelest*—of them all.

I ATE THE APPLE CAKE ALONE IN MY CHAMBERS WHILE READING BY candlelight. I still remember the book. It was *The Iliad,* by Homer. All I wanted was to become lost in the story of the Trojan War and the fate of its heroes. Anything to stop thinking about my brother, the Lion, and Father's fawning lords. After a while, I must have dozed off, only to awaken to sounds coming from Vivian's room. Our chambers were next to one other, and the mortar between the common wall had crumbled in places, allowing me to sometimes hear my brother talking. Yet it was not conversation I heard, but a woman's moans. My brother's grunts mixed with her sighs. As the sounds of their pleasure rose toward a crescendo, bile churned in my gut.

I tried to cover my ears with my pillow when the door to my chamber flew open. My heart jumped.

Odo stood at the threshold, an urgent look on his face. "We have to go, lad," he said in a hushed voice. "Things have taken a foul turn. At the end of the feast, the Lion was told to put down the weaker pup, and it doesn't take a scholar to know what that means."

"You heard this?" I gasped.

"No, but the warning came from someone who did." Odo glanced at the shared wall. "By the sound of things, your brother's a bit preoccupied, so we best go now."

"Are you coming?"

"Aye," Odo replied. "Once they learn I warned you, it won't just be the weaker pup they'll want to put down. We can take refuge in Dordogne with your uncle."

I nodded as a swell of apprehension crashed over me. I quickly pulled on my boots and grabbed my book and whatever clothes I could carry before hurrying from my chamber. Together, we skulked down the stairwell and through a passageway with rushlights still burning in sconces on the wall. When we arrived at the door to the courtyard, Odo paused. "When we reach the stables, saddle your charger and the roan mare for me. I'll take care of the guardsman at the gate."

I sucked in an anxious breath and answered with a nod. Odo opened the door to a rush of the bitter night air. The stables stood fifteen paces from the door beneath the light of a half-moon. "Now, lad," Odo said.

I bolted for the stables and gave a relieved sigh the moment I stepped on the structure's hay-strewn floor. I found my charger's saddle and fumbled with the buckle, all the while praying that Odo would succeed with whatever he planned for the gate guard. As I strapped on the horse's bridle, I heard voices coming from the stable door. I froze. One voice belonged to Odo; the other's was cut short with a loud thud.

"We're clear, lad," Odo said from the stable's shadows. He gripped a wooden mallet used for shoeing horses and stood over one of Father's guardsmen, a fellow named Boen. The guardsman sprawled face-down in the hay. "Asked him to help me cause one of the mares was acting strange," Odo explained. "He'll feel like he drank a barrel of ale in the morning but won't be too worse for the wear. Now we'd best get going."

We walked our horses toward the gate, trying to stay within the shadows of the curtain wall surrounding the courtyard. When we reached the twin timber gates, I helped Odo remove the heavy wooden bar, straining under its weight. With a grunt, Odo pulled the gate open, just as I saw a flare of light out of the corner of my eye. I craned my neck, only to find the doors of the keep wide open and flush with torchlight. "The pup!" a man hollered from the doorway.

Men with swords spilled from the keep, but the burliest among them gripped a hunter's bow. I leaped onto my mount and kicked its ribs. The charger darted forward; an arrow whizzed by my ear. Had the shaft grazed my flesh, I knew I might not staunch the bleeding without a dose of my elixir. In my haste to flee, I'd left the vials in my chamber.

As my charger galloped through the gateway, a second arrow thudded into the timber gate. From the courtyard, the Lion bellowed with rage. "To the kennels! Release the dogs!"

A chorus of barking erupted from the courtyard. I saw the worry in Odo's eyes as my charger caught the steward's mare racing down the road. These weren't the howls of greyhounds but the roaring barks of mastiffs. Dogs large enough to hunt wild boar and strong enough to pull an armored man from his horse.

I gripped my charger's reins, my knuckles turning white. Amid the pounding of hooves, the growling and snarling grew louder. I glanced over my shoulder. Three of the mastiffs barreled toward us, spittle flying from their massive jaws. Without urging, my charger galloped harder, as if sensing the beasts' approach. When I glanced back again, the distance between us and our pursuers had increased. The mastiffs may have been mighty, but they were no match for the speed of our young mounts.

As Aygremont faded from view, my heartbeat began to calm, just as a new tightness formed in my stomach. For I was an exile now, and only God knew if I would ever see my homeland again.

9

DORDOGNE

I
f I had escaped a lion's den in Aygremont, I found a veritable haven in Dordogne.

My uncle, Duke Aymon, lived in a sprawling castle built around the remains of an old Roman tower. Made of golden limestone blocks, the castle stood atop a cliff on the north bank of the Dordogne river. From a window in my chamber, I could look down on the moss-speckled rooftops of the village nestled along the riverbank. In the mornings, men would fish the river, while in the afternoon, children played along its banks. As the end of winter neared, the villagers would tend to the vineyards up and down the hillsides, nurturing the red grapes that produced some of the finest wines in all of Francia.

I spent most of my days in Dordogne with my cousins, two of whom were close to my age. At twenty, Renaud was the oldest, and charming and handsome too, with wavy auburn hair that fell to his shoulders. He was also a horseman of considerable skill, and fiercely competitive. Often I would spend hours with Renaud racing on horseback, hurdling fences, and ring jousting with blunted spears. Renaud's brother, Guichard, was two years his junior and less capable on a horse. But he was far more skilled with his tongue, making wisecracks and japes whenever the moment suited him. Their younger brothers, Richard and Alard, were sandy-haired twins. At fifteen, they were inseparable and even completed each other's sentences. Watching the twins made me envious at times, for Vivian and I had never shared a bond like that. It was nice for once being surrounded by brothers who actually loved one another.

When the twins came of age, Duke Aymon announced it was time they pledged their fealty to the King. So the day after Shrove Tuesday, the duke, his wife, and the twins set out for Paris to arrive at King Pepin's court before the Easter holiday. This left Renaud and Guichard to rule Dordogne, and one of their first official acts was to host a celebration for my twentieth birthday. It began in the castle's Great Hall with a feast of roasted boar and ended over games of dice and far too many carafes of red wine.

Late into the evening, the three of us, along with Odo, lounged in chairs around the dice board. After Odo filled our cups with yet another round of wine, Renaud made an announcement: "I'd wager a year from now," he said with a slur, "we'll be celebrating your birthday in Aygremont."

I wagged a finger. "Vivian won't like that."

"Piss on Vivian," Renaud quipped. "A year from now, he'll be the exile."

"*You*," I replied, "have had too much wine."

"Haven't we all, lad," Odo said, his nose rosy from the drink.

Guichard wiped a drop of wine from his wispy beard. "Too bad your brother didn't follow your father into that hole. He's always been a fool for a pretty lass."

"Ah, yes!" Renaud slapped his knee. "The mystery maiden."

"A woman so unscrupulous she rides naked on a horse!" Guichard added. "Where can I find one like that?"

"She was *practically naked*," I explained. "And I don't think she was a woman."

"Right." Renaud rolled his eyes, waving his hands for effect. "She was one of the Fae."

"Yes," I admitted. "When I found her clothing—if that's what you want to call it—it dissolved in my hand like grains of sand. And the woman and her horse were nowhere to be seen."

Guichard cocked his head. "Are you sure you weren't as drunk then as you are now?"

I shot him a sharp look. "It's sobering to watch your father die. Besides, I know what I saw."

"Say you're right," Renaud said in a more serious tone. "Why would a Fae woman want your father dead? It's not like she knew him."

Odo cleared his throat. "Lads, if you're apt to believe in the Fae, as I do, you'd best remember the old tales. The Fae are wicked creatures. They yearn for chaos and seek to sow it wherever they go." He turned to me. "And that's just what this Fae woman has sown in Aygremont. By starting a bloody war between you and your brother."

I was taken aback by Odo's suggestion. I had never imagined this mysterious woman intentionally starting a war, but that indeed is what she accomplished. But why? Unless grandmother and Odo were right, that the Fae did wicked things for their amusement.

While I was pondering these thoughts, Renaud stood up. "If it's chaos she's sown, then why don't we be the ones to restore some order? Let's end this war before Midsummer."

I shook my head. "What are you saying?"

"That we go on the offensive," Renaud said boldly. "Let's take the fight to Vivian. Guichard and I have hundreds of men at our command, and surely there are lords favorable to our kin who will join our cause. Besides, it's time we proved to Father that we can fight our own battles."

"Are you daft, lad?" Odo asked. "Your father will be furious."

Renaud answered with a wink. "Not if his eldest sons return home as war heroes." He raised his cup. "To the liberation of Aygremont!"

"To the subjugation of Vivian!" Guichard exclaimed.

I felt a warmth in my limbs as I stood up from my chair. No one had ever offered to do something like this before. I tipped my cup as a salt tear stung my eyes. "To the finest cousins a man could have."

Even Odo drank to the toast. Over another carafe of wine, Renaud sketched out a rough battle plan. Then oaths were sworn.

And before midnight, my cousins and I had vowed to go to war.

10

THE BROTHERS' WAR

By the time we set off for battle, I felt the wrong that Vivian had done me might finally be made right.

For one, Renaud and Guichard had mustered a considerable army—three hundred chevaliers from Duke Aymon's lords in Dordogne. Clad in chainmail, they rode chargers and were armed with spears and swords. I too rode a charger, with a long sword sheathed at my belt, strapped at the waist of my new mail hauberk. The hauberk was a birthday gift from my cousins, and it was among the most exquisite coats of armor I had ever seen. Its mail links had been polished to shine like silver, and it even had long sleeves to protect my arms from cuts that might not heal. I wore the hauberk proudly, along with a round helmet and a wooden shield covered in leather and painted with my family's heraldry: a sable field behind the golden leopard of Aygremont. Renaud and Guichard rode in similarly fine armor bearing crimson shields depicting the three crowned lions of Dordogne. Even Odo dressed for war. In his mail coat with a broadsword at his side, the steward looked like a man who had seen his fair share of battles.

Our fortunes improved further when we reached the city of Limoges on the banks of the Vienne River. There, the viscount of

Limoges pledged another hundred chevaliers to our cause. The viscount had long been at odds with Count Bevis, and he viewed Vivian no better. So it did not take much to convince him to march on Aygremont.

Four hundred horsemen left Limoges heading north along the ruins of an old Roman road. Surveying the army my cousins had assembled filled me with an unfamiliar sense of power. I may have been born *mal gist*, but with an army of this size, I had found the antidote to Vivian's raw strength and force of will. Not even Vivian would be bold enough to challenge the combined might of Dordogne and Limoges.

After a full day's ride, our army made camp outside a priory dedicated to a local saint I had never heard of. The monks provided food and ale for Renaud's men, yet after a meeting with the prior, Renaud returned with ill tidings.

"There must have been a spy in Dordogne," Renaud told me. "Vivian has left Aygremont."

I could hardly believe my ears. "He fled?"

"Not quite," Renaud said. "He's gathered his own army and is riding south. If we keep on our path, our armies will meet in the Val d'Anglin."

"That's but a half day's ride," I realized.

A smile spread across Renaud's face. "We wanted a fight. Now we'll have one."

In the Val d'Anglin, our army waited near a hill called Brosse. The horses and their riders stood in two ranks beneath banners bearing the leopard of Aygremont, the lions of Dordogne, and the colorful standards of Limoges and Duke Aymon's lords, all snapping in the wind. The cavalry stretched from the west side of the grassy valley to the east where a dense forest sprawled as far as the eye could see.

Seated on his mare, Odo cast a wary glance toward the forest, which looked as ancient as any I had ever seen. Huge gnarled oaks with twisting branches and moss-covered trunks loomed over wicked brambles while thorny vines filled the spaces between the trees along with shadows that settled deep into the woods.

"If I had my druthers," Odo said, "I wouldn't have stopped here."

Renaud gave the steward a puzzled look. "Why not? Those woods are protecting our eastern flank. This is the perfect place to wait."

Odo shook his head. "That forest is haunted."

"By ghosts?" I asked, gripping my charger's reins.

"Aye," Odo replied. "Men say the forest is as much a graveyard as it is a woodland, and at night, you can hear the spirits of the dead howling like wolves. But there are worse things than ghosts in its shadows, for some men believe this forest belongs to the queen of the dark faeries."

"Then don't go into the woods," Renaud said with a sigh. "Besides, we've no more time for faerie tales. Our company has arrived."

At the valley's north end, another cavalry was emerging from behind the hill. A thicket of spear-tips and banners rose above a horde of war horses and their riders that spanned from one side of the valley to the other. The enemy horsemen must have numbered in the hundreds. A wave of unease roiled my stomach. *Vivian's army is as large as our own!*

Guichard's face went pale. "It's never too late to turn back."

"Nonsense, brother," Renaud said. "It looks like a fair fight."

Vivian's cavalry amassed three hundred yards away, just beyond bowshot. Sunlight glinted off the riders' helmets and mail and caught an array of enemy banners in its glow. The golden leopard of Aygremont adorned the banner fluttering above the head of the army, amid the standards of Vivian's lords on fields of crimson, green, and gold. Yet it was the flag beside Vivian's that sent another wave of bile through my gut. The standard depicted three rams on a blue field beneath a trio of fleurs-de-lis—the banner of the Viscount of Bourges. Vivian had brought a surprise ally, and I knew the horsemen of Bourges would be more than a match for the reinforcements Renaud had picked up in Limoges.

You could taste the tension in the air as our two armies surveyed each other across the battlefield. From the head of Vivian's cavalry, a destrier stepped forward, and its rider thrust out a spear with a black flag tied around its tip. "They seek to parley," Odo observed.

Renaud smiled back. "Then let's parley."

I shared none of my cousin's confidence as I rode with him and the Viscount of Limoges halfway across the field to meet Vivian's envoys. One was the Lion dressed in chainmail over his huntsman's clothes, with his mountain lion cowl in place of a helmet. He glared at me with a contemptuous gaze and a smirk settled on his lips. He was joined by the Viscount of Bourges, a barrel-chested man whose full black beard billowed over the collar of his mail hauberk. His piggish eyes darted between Renaud and me like he was trying to gauge the mettle of his foes. The man who rode between them on a glistening black destrier hid his face behind a fearsome, polished helm. A cross was carved into the metal beneath each eye-hole in the helm as if to boast that its wearer stood on God's side of this conflict. The helm gleamed in the sunlight, along with the rider's mail, which shone like silver against a sable cloak draped over his shoulders. When he reached the middle of the field, the rider, with black-gloved hands, lifted the imposing helm off his head. Vivian stared back. His eyes held an arrogant gleam, and the corners of his mouth curled into a grin. It was not a smile born of brotherly love, but the kind he would make during a hunt when Father would let him kill the stag.

"So, brother," he said, "it has come to this."

I sucked in a feeble breath. "It has."

"And I see our foolhardy cousins have joined you." Vivian glanced around. "I don't see my uncle, Renaud. Does he know you're out here?"

"My brother and I are in charge of Dordogne," Renaud replied.

Vivian feigned a sigh. "So he doesn't know. If any of you survive this, imagine how displeased he will be when he learns what you've done to his precious cavalry."

"Unless we return to Dordogne with your head," Renaud scoffed.

"If you return home at all," Vivian said coldly, "it will be with wounded pride under a cloud of defeat."

"Enough!" I insisted before Renaud could continue their sparring. "You wanted a parley, so what do you have to say?"

"Here are my terms." Vivian leveled his gaze. "Renounce your claim to Aygremont, and my army rides back home. Live in Dordogne if you please, or die there. It matters not to me."

Vivian's words stung. For a moment, the offer seemed worth taking, for the advantage we had hoped to have against his army had melted away like the snow after the first hint of spring. Yet with everything my cousins had done for me, could I truly let them down? *No.* I swallowed hard. "I won't do that."

Vivian clenched his jaw. "You've always been the weak one, brother. We both know how this will end." As if punctuating his words, Vivian wheeled his mount, cradling his silver helm in his left arm as he headed back toward his army. The Viscount of Bourges followed, but the Lion lingered for a breath. He winked at me as his lips stretched into a brown-toothed grin. A chill crawled down my skin.

As our rivals rode off, Renaud stood in his saddle. "Vivian, I'd call you a whoreson if I didn't know your mother! But you're still a bastard at heart!"

Vivian answered with a dismissive wave. By the time he rejoined his men, the butterflies in my stomach had settled into a painful knot. Vivian's words had sown doubt, and I feared I was not strong enough to survive the coming fight.

Two hundred yards across the field from Vivian's army, Renaud commanded his horsemen to form two lines, one behind the other. Astride my charger, I positioned myself in the front line between Odo and Guichard. My leopard banner fluttered overhead in the breeze. Around us, some of the horsemen muttered prayers to saints, while others tightened the leather chinstraps on their helmets. A few swore curses at the opposing cavalry, while a man in the rank behind me retched violently.

My hands were shaking as I fumbled with the stopper to my vile of elixir. I downed the tart liquid in a single gulp, hoping that if I were to get cut, the medicine might keep the wound from bleeding with abandon. When we had set out on this campaign, I had expected a siege of Aygremont, followed by a bloodless surrender. Not a cavalry assault against my brother's army.

I had never taken part in a cavalry charge, and I dreaded the thought of it now. As the ranks of horsemen kicked their mounts into a canter, my heart drummed with the rhythm of their hoofbeats. By the time the horses broke into a full gallop, my heart threatened to pound from my chest.

The surrounding air filled with the chorus of the charge: the chink of mail, the slap of leather, the thunder of hooves, and the battle cries of men. Beside Guichard, Renaud raised his spear. "For God and Saint Pierre!" His men answered with a roar, and I found the battle cry bursting from my lips.

"For God and Saint Pierre!"

Ahead, Vivian's cavalry charged toward us like an unyielding wave. The oncoming horsemen lowered their spears. Clutching my shield's handle with my left hand, I set my spear, fighting to steel my nerves. The ground quaked beneath the horses' hooves. As our two cavalries continued on their course, I clenched my jaw and braced for impact.

The cavalries collided with a boom like a thunderclap that shuddered through my bones. A spear smashed into my shield, jolting me backward. And then the world around me erupted into chaos. A nearby horse fell to an enemy spear, throwing its rider, who was trampled beneath the rain of hooves. Steel clashed against the willow boards of shields. Men cried in rage and pain, and the air misted with blood.

I swung my spear in a wild arc only to have its shaft severed by a sword blade. The attacker pressed on, hammering his longsword. I caught it with my shield, but the blow sent a shudder of pain up my arm. I ripped my sword from its sheath, just as Odo drove a spear through the attacker's side, toppling the rider from his mount. Odo pulled his horse away as another charger crashed to the ground, a spear between its ribs. Horses screamed, and so did men. I sliced my sword at another rider; the blade scraped across the man's shield. I jerked my charger back, a breath before the man's sword glanced off the mail covering my left arm. Renaud's sword scythed through my attacker's neck, his blood splattering my cheek.

"Keep fighting cousin!" Renaud cried before ramming his blade into another horseman's side. I looked for the nearest foe; then a sudden impact nearly threw me from my saddle. Another horse had plowed into my own while crashing to the ground. The wounded beast thrashed on its side, kicking its leg and driving my panicked charger into a mass of horsemen and clanging steel. A sword hacked into my shield, causing the willow boards to crack. I struck back wildly as the cries of men filled my ears, and I could no longer tell friend from foe amid the storm of battle. Then a horrifying new sound joined the battle roar—the fierce barking of mastiffs.

A horde of war dogs barreled into the crowd of horses and men. A mastiff pulled a rider clean from his saddle; another grabbed a horseman by the leg, threatening to tear off the man's limb. A breath caught in my throat. I knew I had to move, but my whole body felt frozen by the fear of the mastiffs' sudden attack.

If our armies had been equal, the Lion's mastiffs tipped the scales. I imagined the stabbing pain of a dog's teeth sinking into my thigh and the weight of its crushing jaws wrenching me from my mount. It would be a horrible way to die, flailing on the ground in the mud and shite with a mastiff tearing out your throat. Then someone grabbed my shoulder. I turned to find Odo pulling me from the fray. "Fall back, lad!"

His words startled me into action. I spurred my charger, guiding it toward a stream of Renaud's horsemen fleeing the battle. Beside me, a leaping mastiff took down another rider; the dog's snarls drowned out the man's screams.

"Keep moving, lad!" Odo hollered.

I rode as hard as I could. On his mare, Odo kept pace. "Head south at the tree line—" His words ended with a cry of pain as an arrow shaft protruded from his shoulder.

I glanced back in horror to see the Lion taking aim from the saddle of his horse. He pulled the string of his hunter's bow and loosed a shaft. The arrow sped forward and punched into the flank of my charger. The horse let out a whinnying cry as a second arrow pierced its ribs. I felt my entire world tipping to the side as the charger's legs gave way, sending the beast tumbling to the ground. I leaped from the saddle and crashed into the turf, rolling away a breath before my charger nearly crushed me.

I looked up as another shaft sank into Odo's side. From the saddle of his mare, the old steward gasped. "Use your wits and run!"

I scrambled to my feet, only to hear hooves bearing down. I reached for my sword, but it was gone, lying useless a yard from my fallen charger. I looked up into the eyes of a massive bay stallion. Reigning in the horse, its rider wore no mail but a green cloak and cowl. The horseman pulled the hood free, revealing a head of raven-colored hair. Staring down at me was no horseman at all, but a bright-eyed girl, close in age to my own. "Get on!" she demanded.

"Who are you?" I gasped.

"The last person you'll ever see if you keep sitting there like a target."

One of the Lion's arrows slammed into the turf three feet away, jolting me to my feet. Another shaft whizzed by my side.

"Hurry!" she cried.

I leaped onto the stallion, only to find the girl was riding it bareback. As she tugged the beast's reins, I glanced back at Odo. Slumped in his saddle, the steward was clutching his wounded side and staring slack-jawed at the girl.

As if he was looking at a ghost.

11

THE LION

I wrapped my arms around the girl's waist as she drove her stallion toward the forest. For an instant, I thought of Odo's warnings about those haunted woods, but then the mastiffs' barks returned my thoughts to the urgency of our situation. As I glanced over my shoulder, my stomach tightened into a knot. Less than a bowshot away, four mastiffs charged after us, urged on by the Lion mounted on his steed.

"Bayard," the girl whispered into the stallion's ear, "to the glade."

The stallion galloped toward a gap between two ancient-looking oaks overgrown with vines. I had to duck below thick, gnarled branches as the horse leaped into the breach, pounding its way through a twisted labyrinth of trees. The horse maneuvered around broad tree trunks and bramble bushes, and over tree roots covered with toadstools, as if it had raced through the forest a hundred times before. Clinging to the girl, I glanced up for a moment. Only slivers of sunlight pierced the web of spidery branches that formed a dense canopy over the forest, and the light grew dimmer still as the horse careened down the shadowy tunnels between the trees. I only hoped the mastiffs would become lost in the leafy maze.

The stallion slowed and cantered through a seam between two

trees. We emerged into a glade thick with the smell of damp earth and dead leaves. "You can let go now," the girl said.

I had not realized how tightly I had been holding onto her. "Right." I unclasped my arms. The girl slid off the stallion's back and landed nimbly on the forest duff. Seeing her stand for the first time, I was struck by how slender she was. And pretty too.

The girl gave a sharp nod toward the ground. "Oh," I replied, grasping what she meant. I climbed off the stallion's back, dropping to the ground with a crunch of leaves. In the distance, the mastiffs' barking had grown faint, and I wondered if the stallion had lost them.

"I must thank you," I said. "But I don't even know your name."

"You can call me Angelica."

"Why are you trying to save me, Angelica?"

"Because, Maugis d'Aygremont, my liege wants you very much alive."

I was stunned that she knew who I was. I did not recall ever seeing this girl before, and it was hard to fathom that someone had sent her to find me, particularly some nobleman. Between the drab-colored dress she wore beneath her cloak and the soft leather shoes on her feet, she looked as nondescript as a village girl. "You serve a lord?"

"Everyone serves someone," she said, "and the someone I serve has high hopes for you."

I scratched the side of my head, struggling to imagine why this mysterious nobleman had taken such an interest in me. "What's your lord's name?"

Before she could answer, a loud barking blared through the forest. Any hope I had of escaping the mastiffs quickly vanished.

Angelica scraped a hand through her hair. "They've picked up our scent." She turned to the stallion. "Bayard, try to lead some of them away. Meet us at the brook." The horse nodded back. As it headed into the woods, Bayard stomped his hoofs hard, leaving visible hoofprints in the damp earth.

I shook my head in disbelief. "That horse understands what you just said?"

"You'd be surprised how much Bayard knows," she said. "Now, let's get moving. We have to deal with these dogs."

Angelica darted back into the woods. "What are you doing?" I asked, following her. "You plan to lose them in there?"

She glanced back. "Will you ever stop asking questions?" She padded down a narrow pathway between the trees. Mushrooms sprang between the roots, and creepers choked the trunks and covered the tree branches, dripping with hanging vines. Halfway down the path, she stopped. From the direction of the glade, the barking grew louder.

"Why are we stopping," I asked incredulously.

"Enough with the questions." She shook her head, then pulled an object from her robes. Between her fingers, it looked as large a hazelnut, but rather than being brown in color, it was opaque like a crystal. She put the crystal to her lips and whispered an odd-sounding word. *"Eoh."* I jumped back when the crystal flared with light, before settling into a soft yet brilliant white glow.

"How did you do that?" I asked, blinking.

She held up a finger. "Shush."

The sound of paws tearing through dead leaves mixed with the mastiff's snarls as two of the enormous dogs burst through a gap between the trees. I held back a cry and reached for Angelica, but she brushed my hand away. Raising the crystal, she uttered a series of words, neither Latin nor Frankish. The crystal flared again. The mastiffs stopped snarling, their eyes fixed on the light. As the lead mastiff sauntered toward her, she reached out and scratched the top of the dog's massive head. I could hardly believe my eyes.

Angelica snapped her fingers and pointed to the woods to her left. "Go," she commanded. The dogs darted away, disappearing into the shadows beneath the vine-laden branches. Angelica moved to follow them, though I just stood there. My mind struggled to comprehend what had happened. A moment ago, the savage mastiffs had hauled armored men from their horses and ripped out their throats. Yet around Angelica, with her glowing stone and strange words, they were as docile as house pets.

A part of my brain told me this could not be real, but then a gruff voice called out from the entrance to the glade. "Seems I've found you, your lordship."

The sound of the Lion's voice sent a stab of fear through my chest. I felt frozen in place as the Lion stepped from the shadows between two trees. He held his bow waist high with an arrow nocked on the string. "Looks like the battle's not gone your way," he said with a grim smile. "Such a pity."

I knew that even if I tried to run, he'd put an arrow in my back before I could finish my first stride. I gave a hopeless glance to Angelica, who crouched behind the base of an oak five paces away. Faint light spilled from beneath her palm against one of the thick vines wrapped around the trunk. "Keep him talking," she whispered.

I must have looked at her like she was touched in the head. "Do it!" she hissed.

Reluctantly, I turned back toward the Lion, my eyes drawn to the steel tip of the arrow-head he could put through my heart with the pull of his bowstring.

"What's wrong boy," the Lion called down the pathway. "The cat got your tongue?"

Uncertain what to do, I slowly held up my hands. Angelica had prevailed against the mastiffs, and I had no hope but to listen to her now. So I spoke the only words I could think of. "Odulf, it doesn't have to be this way," I said. "You served my father for years. Hunted with him, and with me, for years. Why not serve both his sons now?"

"I knew your father better than most," the Lion snarled. "If he'd had a breath left in him as he lay in that pit, I'm sure he would have wanted only one of his sons to rule Aygremont. So look at it this way —I'm about to fulfill your late father's dying wish."

In the branches overhead, I glimpsed a flicker of blueish light. Within its eerie glow, something was moving. My eyes grew wide, and once again, I could not believe what I was seeing. The creepers and vines had come alive, writhing through the treetops. The sight of a thing so unnatural sent a chill crawling down my skin, and it took all my will to contain my fear and keep my focus on the Lion.

"Odulf," I pleaded, "think about what you're doing. You're not a murderer."

"Of course I am, boy. I'm a hunter, and you're my quarry." The Lion's eyes narrowed. He raised his bow, aiming straight for my chest. "This one's from your brother."

My gaze darted from the arrow to the vines descending toward the Lion's head like a brood of vipers. As the Lion pulled back his bowstring, the vines, in unison, made a serpent-like strike and wrapped around the huntsman's neck. The Lion gave a startled scream; the arrow thunked harmlessly into the duff. His hands flew to the vines, which twisted like a thick noose around his neck. His face turned red as the vines recoiled toward the treetops, lifting him off his feet. Flailing, his legs kicked violently until I heard a crack as the noose of vines crushed his throat. His hands, clinging to the vines, lost their grip. His limbs no longer twitched, and my would-be killer swayed lifelessly from the trees like a condemned man hanging from the gallows.

THE LEOPARD

Beside the tree, Angelica brushed off her palms like a farmer after a day's work. A ghost of a smile touched her lips. As I stared at her, the reality of what had happened began to sink in. *She just killed the Lion ...*

I felt a sudden swell of dread. *The forest belongs to the queen of the dark faeries,* Odo had said. Could Angelica be one of them? The thought assailed half my mind, but the other half—the rational part— did not want to believe it. Angelica was nothing like the Fae woman who had caused my father's death. The Fae woman was unlike any real woman I had ever beheld, ageless in appearance with features far too perfect for a mortal being. Even her hair was unnatural, shining like spun silver. Angelica, however, appeared to be a normal girl of twenty or so years, with dark hair like many other women in Francia. And when I had held onto her during the ride through the forest, her chest heaved when she breathed, like any other person made of flesh and blood. But if she was not one of them, how could she do these things? *Unless...*

The question slipped from my mouth. "Are you a witch?"

Angelica shot me a scowl. "That's a nasty word. I just saved your life for the second time today, and all I get is an insult?"

"I'm grateful, but what you just did ..."

"Is *not* witchcraft," she insisted. "You shouldn't talk about things you don't understand, Maugis."

I ran my fingers nervously through my hair. Our priest at Aygremont had preached that magic came from demons, and what other than magic could explain what she had done. "But that light..."

"Is summoned from the soul."

Back then, I had never heard of anyone summoning light from their soul. The whole notion of it seemed contrary to everything the Church had taught me in my youth. Magic was evil, pure and simple. There was no middle ground. "If it's not witchcraft, then how did you do it?"

"The power," she said, tapping the side of her head, "comes from in here. You just have to know how to use it." She stepped through a gap between the trees, gesturing me to follow. "Are you coming, or are you just going to stand there gaping at me?"

At that moment, I did not know whether to believe her. After what I'd seen her do, half my mind urged me to run away. But she had saved my life twice now, and despite everything the priests had taught us about magic and witches, I wanted to believe her. "Where will we go?" I asked.

"To find Bayard."

I let out a relieved sigh. "So we can escape, right?"

"Something like that." She glanced over her shoulder. "But we need to hurry. The Lion may have arrived first, but the leopard won't be far behind. This time, your brother will want to make sure to put down the weaker pup."

My mouth fell slack. "My brother said that once, but how did you know?"

"I know a lot of things," she said with a coy smile. "Now make haste."

I did not know what to think of this woman, yet the notion of Vivian hunting me in these woods like a prized stag was incentive enough to move swiftly—until a pang of guilt rooted me in place. I had almost forgotten about Odo, left wounded on the battlefield. And what of Renaud and Guichard? I had not seen either of them fall during the battle, but that was before the mastiffs attacked. I prayed that they had fled and survived, and that I would see them again in Dordogne. For where else was there to go?

"Changing your mind?" Angelica asked, annoyed.

"No," I said. "I was thinking about my cousins and my friend Odo."

Angelica reached out and took my hand; the touch of her fingers sent a tingle up my arm. "Your cousin, Renaud, is a renowned warrior," she said gently. "He'll find a way to survive and keep his brother alive too. Your steward was alive when we left him. There's always hope."

Still holding my hand, she urged me to go with her. "I hope you're right," I replied.

The tunnels beneath the canopy of branches and overgrown vines twisted and turned, yet Angelica maneuvered through them like she had been here before. Soon, I heard the trickle of a stream. Through the branches, I spied Bayard drinking from a brook that snaked between the trees.

The massive stallion looked up as Angelica approached him. "Did you have any trouble with the dogs?"

Bayard shook his head. There was not a scratch on his glistening hide. Angelica caressed his cheek, and Bayard nuzzled her arm.

"He truly knows what you're saying?" I asked.

Bayard made a loud snort and glared at me.

"He knows what you're saying too," Angelica said. "If you insult his intelligence, you'll make him mad."

Bayard craned his neck, his ears twitching.

"Do you hear men?" Angelica asked.

Bayard nodded.

"They're coming, we have to move." She patted Bayard and started down the path cut by the brook. The stallion followed behind her.

Though I could not tell east from west among the tangle of trees, I had a feeling she was heading deeper into the woods, which sent a quiver through my stomach. But then I heard voices in the opposite direction. One was Vivian's, but there were more—many more. The unease in my stomach hardened into a rock.

For Vivian was coming, and a hunting party was coming with him.

~

I HURRIED AFTER ANGELICA AND BAYARD. THE SHADOWS BETWEEN THE trees grew darker with each stride. The twisting branches, thick with moss, blocked out the sky, creating a dusk-like gloom that threatened to fade into night.

I jumped at the sound of something darting through the forest, crackling through branches and brambles as it moved. Yet in the twisting maze of trees, I couldn't tell where it came from. Or what it was, for the crunch of leaves between our feet and Bayard's hooves mixed with the sound of whatever beasts lurked in the bowels of this place. I reached for my sword but found it missing from my side. Swearing under my breath, I remembered the blade lying beyond reach on the battlefield when Angelica saved me. My dagger would be my only weapon now. I pulled it from its sheath.

As we traipsed deeper into the forest, the gloom thickened, and moss hung like cobwebs between the branches. "Do you know where you're going?" I asked under my breath.

"Of course," Angelica hissed over her shoulder.

Her words did little to calm my nerves. "Shouldn't we be escaping?"

"I know what I'm doing," she insisted, before ducking into a seam between two gnarled oaks and disappearing into the shadows. Bayard glared at me with his big brown eyes, then followed Angelica. But I hesitated.

"Are you coming?" Angelica called out in a hushed tone.

I swallowed hard and stepped into the seam. I found myself in a narrow glade, where Angelica and Bayard waited. On the opposite side of the glade, a damp curtain of mist hung between the trees. The sight of it made me scratch my head. There had not been a hint of rain in the air before the battle. But I felt a dampness in the air now, and something else, like the calm before a violent storm. I walked to the curtain of mist and brushed it with my fingers. The vapor was wet to the touch, but I swore I sensed a subtle thrum in the air when my fingers passed through it. Odo's words about these woods crept back into my thoughts. *That forest is haunted.*

I turned to Angelica. "Where have you taken us?"

Angelica sighed. "Maugis, you have to trust me."

I wanted to trust her, but Odo's warnings were churning through my brain. As I glanced at the mist, hanging there like some unnatural barrier, a wave of nausea washed through my gut. "No," I muttered, "this doesn't feel right."

Shaking my head, I backed away from the mist.

"Maugis, wait." Angelica reached for me, but I bolted from the glade.

Cold sweat beaded on my forehead, and my heart pounded in my chest. I fled through the forest, but a breath caught in my throat when I heard the chink of mail and the crunch of leaves beneath leather boots. I froze and glanced toward the sound. Armored men with drawn swords were stalking through the woods—Vivian's men, and enough to surround the glade. I crept backward. My foot landed on a fallen branch; it snapped loud enough to stop Vivian's men in their tracks.

"There!" One of the men pointed in my direction.

The only way out was the way I had come. Vivian's men charged forward, hacking through vines and brambles with their swords in their furious attempt to seize their prey. I darted away toward the glade. I burst through a thicket of trees to find Angelica and Bayard still there, just as a half-dozen mail-clad men stepped from the surrounding woods. My pursuers arrived next, adding five more men to the semi-circle of soldiers. From among the warriors, sauntered Vivian. In his left arm, he cradled his polished helm, streaked with blood from the battle.

His gaze ranged from me to Angelica. Then his eyes widened. "Angelica?"

I could not believe my ears.

"I left you at the camp," Vivian said, shaking his head.

"I ran away," Angelica replied defiantly.

"For him?" Vivian's words dripped with contempt.

"It didn't take long after you claimed me as your mistress," Angelica said, "before I recognized Maugis was the worthier ruler of Aygremont."

I gasped. Her slender legs, her raven-colored hair—the realization struck me like a blow. The woman from the funeral, the one who had shared my brother's bed...

Anger rose in Vivian's brow. "You ungrateful whore! You'll get your due, but first, there are family matters to attend to." His eyes settled on the dagger still clutched in my hand, then he chuckled. "Only you, brother, would bring a knife to a sword fight. But then again, you always were the weaker of the two of us."

My knees began to tremble. "Let her go, Vivian," I pleaded. "You've won the fight. If she's free to go, then I'll surrender."

Vivian's lips spread into a cruel smile. "Angelica is my business, not yours. And you are in no position to bargain, brother. I need more than surrender. I need you to renounce your claim to Aygremont. Do so, and we can be again like family. You'll have a place at my table. You can join my hunt and take whatever mistress you may fancy. Just not her."

A look of alarm flashed across Angelica's face. "Maugis, don't do it! Before the battle, they discussed what would happen if you surrendered. They swore to kill you so that no man could question Vivian's claim."

"Shut her up!" Vivian roared.

Two of his soldiers started toward Angelica. With an angry snort, Bayard reared up on his hind legs, blocking their path. One of the men raised his sword, but Bayard was quicker. His left hoof smashed into the first man's helmet, and with a sickening thud, the soldier crumpled to the turf. The right hoof struck the other soldier in the chest. Ribs cracked like dry twigs, and with a gasp, the man collapsed.

Then chaos erupted in the glade. Four of the mail-clad soldiers lunged at me as Angelica screamed.

"Maugis, hide in the mists!"

As the men came for me, I did the only thing I could think to do—listen to Angelica. So I fled into the mists.

13

THE BONEYARD

I felt a murmur in the air as the wet mists washed over me. The fog was bitter against my skin, like a winter frost.

Even though the mist obscured my vision, I ran, knowing Vivian's men would pursue me. My boots crunched something brittle beneath them. Acorns, I imagined—an instant before my knee hit something solid. I fell forward and landed on a gnarled lump of tree roots so hard it forced the air from my lungs and sent my dagger clattering into the mists.

Grimacing in pain, I searched for my pursuers, but I could see little. The tree trunks were but shadows in the murk and all around me were stump-like shapes as if woodsmen had harvested this part of the forest. I reached for the one I had tripped over. My hand touched damp moss and something beneath it. Something smooth, unlike the bark of a tree.

I brought my face closer to the object, then gasped. Staring back was a human skull with mushrooms growing out of its eye sockets. The skeleton was hunched over, clutching itself in death, moss clinging to its bones, with vines growing over its legs and in between its ribs. I stifled a scream. For surrounding the skeleton were not acorns and forest duff, but bones, some vaguely human, others belonging to animals, strewn across the ground. Another nearby stump took on a vaguely human shape, and Odo's warning slammed into my mind. *That forest is haunted...* I fought a wave of panic—*and Angelica sent me here!*

The clamor of men forced my thoughts back to my immediate situation.

"It's a bloody boneyard," one of the men said, fear in his voice.

"Get hold of yourself," another chided. "Maybe a battle was fought here a long time ago. Just find the pup. We'll add him to the corpses."

Vivian's men were but silhouettes in the gray haze, but the chink of mail and the sound of boots crushing frail bones made the breath stick in my throat.

The man wandered through the boneyard, peering through the mist. When his gaze found me, his mouth widened into a grin. "I've got you, pup."

Fear pulsed through my veins, then my eyes flew wide. A skeletal hand reached from behind the man and wrapped around his mouth. Hunched in death a moment ago, the skeleton behind my pursuer rose to its full height. Its other hand struck at the man's throat, pressing bony fingers into his flesh. The vines around the skeleton's leg began slithering like snakes, entangling the man's legs and wrenching him to the ground. He flailed as the skeleton bore down, tightening its grip on the man's neck and muffling his panicked cries.

Sweet Jesus! My mind screamed as I watched the shadowy forms of other men wrestling with the dead as if the entire boneyard had come to life. I staggered away; the screams of men echoed through the forest.

As I streaked past more moss-covered skeletons slumped against trees and curled into mounds overgrown with toadstools, I feared their bony claws reaching for my legs. Huffing for breath, I found myself in another glade awash with swirling mists. In its center stood another pile of mossy bones, perhaps three or four skeletons clinging to one another when they had died. To my relief, the skeletons did not move, though one held an object as if he were offering it to someone. I padded toward the macabre sight, breath heaving from my chest. The foremost skeleton was offering a sword with a cross-shaped hilt, and not an inch of it seemed touched by the moss that speckled the skeleton's yellowish bones. Both the pommel and cross-guard were plated in gold, and its blade shone like polished silver. I stepped closer to the weapon, I could almost reach out and touch it. A pattern of engraved letters flowed like scrollwork down the length of the blade. It was the finest sword I had ever laid eyes upon. Only the holler of a man tore my gaze from the weapon.

"Brother!" Vivian called from somewhere in the mists. "You cannot hide in here forever!" There was violence in his voice and something else. *Determination.*

Without a second thought, I reached for the sword. Metal scraped against hardened bone as I pulled it from the skeleton's grasp. Yet there was more to the sound, as if the blade had whispered its name. *Durendal...*

The weight of the sword pulled my arm toward the ground. I struggled to lift it with two hands, just as a shadowy form approached the glade.

My muscled tensed. Vivian emerged through the mists. He had discarded his polished helm and gripped his longsword with both hands, pointing it menacingly toward me. He glared at me with cold, hard eyes.

"Hello, brother." Vivian's nostrils flared as he spoke. "I don't know how you found this place, or what you did to scare away my men, but I'm not so easily deterred."

"The dead," I insisted, "they came alive."

"I saw no such thing," Vivian scoffed.

I knew what I had seen. *The skeletons had risen to life; how could Vivian have missed them?* As he crept closer, I shook off the thought

I raised the sword chest high, though my arms trembled with its weight.

"I see you found a blade," Vivian sneered, "and a fine one at that. But it looks a tad heavy, brother, in your feeble hands."

I ignored the insult. "Where's Angelica?"

"She fled behind that nasty stallion. But when I'm done with you,

I'll find her and punish her for her betrayal. And then I'll feed her horse to my hounds."

My spirits soared, knowing that Angelica had escaped. But then a troubling thought crept into my mind. What if the skeletons had been her doing? After what she had done to the Lion, anything was possible. *But if she could summon the dead to do her bidding, why would she leave Vivian alive?*

My brother took another step forward, his blade at the ready. I knew the time for questions was over. I thought of dropping the heavy sword and running away. But there seemed no escape from this mist-filled forest, and Vivian was an exceptional hunter. Though a duel was just as bad, if not worse. While father had trained both of us in swordplay since we were boys, Vivian was faster and stronger, and far more adept with a blade.

"Must we do this?" I asked desperately.

"Yes," Vivian hissed. Then, with a bellow of rage, he struck.

14

TO THE DEATH

I raised my sword an instant before Vivian's would have sliced into my chest. Steel clanged against steel like the peal of a bell, and the blow shuddered through my arms to the bones. I staggered back as Vivian lunged again. This time I hammered my sword on top of Vivian's blade, glancing it to the side. Vivian followed with a backhand swing, and my parry missed its mark. His sword scraped across my mailed shoulder, shearing into the chain metal, followed by the sting of steel biting flesh.

I cried out as I leaped back. Blood was pooling beneath my rent mail, and I knew the bleeding might not stop. Vivian's eyes burned with the triumph of striking first blood.

"Vivian," I pleaded. "Be rational, we can talk this through."

"You sealed your fate, brother," Vivian growled, "the moment you brought an army against me!" He punctuated his words with a violent strike. His sword clanged against mine, and the force of the blow quaked through my hands.

As he advanced, I stepped back, quick enough to dodge a wild swing of his blade. "You became a dead man," he vowed, "the moment I found you with her!" He followed with an arching blow that slammed against my sword so hard it nearly tore the weapon from my grip.

Vivian's eyes flared. "My whore, did she sleep with you?" My sword caught his next strike, but each of his assaults was coming with greater force. "Is that what made you feel like a man? Man enough to challenge me!" The following blow rammed my blade into my chest and almost knocked me from my feet.

"Or did you sleep with her to take something that belonged to me?" The look in his eyes turned from rage to madness. He made a wild swing. I scampered backward to avoid the blow, and Vivian nearly lost his footing. For an instant, he was exposed, and had I been a true swordsman, I could have run him through. But I had no desire to kill him.

The insult of my inaction only fueled his fury. "You always wanted what I had—my strength, Father's favor!"

I parried his next attack but knew I could not match his rage. My heart drummed in my chest; my lungs gasped for breath.

"And now you," Vivian huffed, "you want Aygremont!" He roared as he swung. My sword met his, but the impact spun me to the side.

Vivian lunged. His blade sliced across my unprotected thigh, and I howled as pain seared through my leg.

My brother drew back and flashed a feral grin, like a hunter who's cornered his prey. It was the same look the Lion had had when he pulled his bowstring. "Aygremont is mine," Vivan snarled. "Angelica is mine. It's all mine!"

As I stood there like a wounded deer, Odo's last words flashed through my skull. *Use your wits and run!* I was never going to out-duel my brother, so I did the only thing I could think to do. With all my might, I flung Durendal at his head.

Vivian had not expected that move. He tried to block the spinning blade, but Durendal clattered off his sword and glanced against his cheek. Vivian winced as blood sprayed from the wound.

I bolted from the glade. With each stride, my injured thigh pulsed with pain.

"For that, I will make you suffer!" Vivian bellowed.

Ahead, I found a path through the woods. Mist swirled around the trail, forming an eerie tunnel with only the shadows of tree trunks lining its sides. I flew down the path as fast as my wounded leg would allow. Behind me, I heard Vivian crash into the forest duff. "God's bones!" he cursed.

I glanced back to see him sprawled onto the ground with his foot caught behind a tree root. His cheeks flushed with anger. I willed myself to move faster.

As I fled, I realized Vivian should have finished me the instant after he had wounded my leg. Yet he had drawn back. His jealous hatred must have clouded his mind, for why else would he have toyed with his prey?

I heard Vivian's boots pounding down the path, only to realize the ground had changed beneath my feet. Instead of a carpet of dead leaves and small bones, I tread over hard-packed earth cracked with tiny fissures. Before me, I could no longer see the shadows of trees within the gloom, nor was I still within the misty tunnel that stretched through the forest. It was as if the tunnel had emptied into a mist-filled plain. The murk appeared more like an evening fog billowing throughout this strange place.

Still, I ran. Though the pain in my thigh was nearly unbearable. I glanced back. The forest had ended, for in the distance, stood the shadow of the tree line through which Vivian entered onto the barren plain. A trail of my blood spanned the distance between us, which could not have been more than fifty paces.

"Maugis!" Vivian called with venom in his voice. A smear of blood ran from his cheek to his jaw. "I could just let you bleed to death. But where's the sport in that?"

With every stride, blood oozed from my wounded thigh. I could feel the weakness creeping into my limbs. Ahead, the silhouette of something broader than a barn, and enormously tall, loomed through the fog. If the structure was inhabited, whoever lived there could offer sanctuary. Yet I knew I would never make it to the door. The wound had hobbled my leg to the point I was dragging it behind me.

Though nothing deterred Vivian. He stalked toward me, gripping his bloodstained sword. He glared at me with his hunter's gaze, but I looked aside. That's when I noticed the movement in the fog. They were but shadows, human in shape, except for one. It was a great four-legged creature that moved with the grace of a stallion. *Bayard*.

Just ten paces away, Vivian gave a satisfied smile. "They say the wounded animal is the most dangerous, but it looks like there's no more fight left in you, brother."

"He'll fight for me," called a woman's voice. As I turned toward the sound, Angelica emerged from the fog. Beyond her, the horse-shaped shadow cantered within the murk.

Vivian grimaced. "This is too rich. Now you can watch him die. And by the time I'm done with you, you'll wish you could join him."

"Maugis!" Angelica cried as Vivian stepped toward me, baring his teeth. He raised his blade for the kill.

My limbs froze, but Odo's last words screamed in my mind. *Use your wits!* I glanced at the shadows in the mists. "Bayard," I yelled, "he wants to hurt her and feed you to his hounds!"

The gigantic stallion burst through the fog, his hooves thundering across the hard ground. Vivian gasped at the charging warhorse. He tried to leap away, but Bayard moved too fast. Lowering his massive head, the stallion smashed into Vivian. My brother was thrown forward, flailing like a rag doll. He landed on the hard ground. With a look of terror, he raised his arms, a breath before Bayard trampled him beneath his hooves.

The stallion wheeled around as my brother lay motionless on the plain. I glanced at Angelica. A devilish smile spread across her face. Then, with a sudden rush like a blast of wind, the fog burned away. The scattering haze revealed a dozen warriors surrounding us. I sucked in a breath as I realized they were not men but women decked in silver helms and tight-fighting mail. All of them, except one. She stood taller than the rest in a white silken gown, and her silver hair spilled over her shoulders. As she glided beside Angelica, I found myself staring at her face, both beautiful and ageless.

The face of the woman who had killed my father.

15

THE FAE

The ground felt unsteady under my feet. I had just killed my brother, only to find myself staring at the woman who had murdered my father. The woman who started this war between brothers. My mind reeled at the implication—had I become her unwitting pawn?

I staggered backward. Angelica rushed to catch me, but I pushed her away. The effort sent a surge of pain up my leg that dropped me to a knee. My hand fell to my wounded thigh, slick with blood. "Is this your liege?" I asked Angelica. "She killed my father, and you were her servant." Anger swelled within my chest and cracked my voice. "You lured me here, and for what? To make me kill my brother?"

Angelica fell silent and glanced toward the silver-haired woman. As the woman stepped forward, I knew I gazed upon the object of Odo's warnings. The ruler of this forest. The queen of the dark faeries.

Despite her ethereal beauty, there was an edge to her presence. As in nature, where the most beautiful serpents are the ones with the deadliest venom. When she spoke, I sensed a whisper in the air, as if her voice could command the wind. "I am Orionde," she said, "and I did not kill your father. His lust did. Had he not chased after me, he would still be lord of Aygremont."

"But you knew he would follow you," I insisted. "It was a trap."

"Your father made a choice," Orionde replied, "and his character influenced that choice. Your brother was no different. Instead of lust, it was his hatred and his jealousy that drove him into the forest to hunt you down like one of his stags. He could have let you flee with Angelica, but he made a different decision. He would have killed you, had you not stopped him."

I pressed my hands against my cheeks, struggling to comprehend what she was telling me. I doubted the truth of her words, for Odo had warned of the Fae's wickedness. And there were more Fae here than the one who called herself Orionde. The female warriors surrounding us had the same ageless beauty and dangerous presence. They stood on the barren plain in the shadow of a tower hundreds of feet high that appeared hewn from reddish stone. I had never looked upon a spire so tall. It should have towered over the treetops and been visible for a league in every direction. But I had seen no sight of it when we had approached the Val d'Anglin.

I drew in a deep breath. If I had fallen into their trap, I had nothing left to lose. My brother lay lifeless, and I was bleeding to death from the wound on my thigh. All I wanted were answers. "You were waiting for us. If you wanted Vivian dead, you could have done it. Just like you killed his men in the boneyard."

"No." Orionde narrowed her gaze. "You had to be the one to defeat him. It was the only way for you to win back your lands and become the true and rightful count of Aygremont."

"Had he died of any cause, I would be the sole lord of Aygremont."

"Not in the hearts of men," she explained. "You would have inherited your title because of mishaps that befell your father and brother. Few of the King's men would respect a lord who earned his title that way. But, you—you defeated Vivian in battle, and men will remember that. Some may even sing songs of it."

I grimaced. "Why in God's name does my reputation matter to you?"

JOSEPH FINLEY

"Because it will matter to the man who will be King." Orionde looked at me with a stern gaze. "He shall unite Europe and lead it out of the dark ages that have gripped these lands since the fall of Rome. He will forge an empire where knowledge and learning can thrive again and the most sacred truths can be preserved until the time when they will be needed. Legend will revere him as Charlemagne. Though in this age, he is Charles, the eldest son of King Pepin. Yet once he claims his throne, he will surround himself with twelve peers, like the twelve apostles, and you must be foremost among them."

My mouth hung open as she spoke. "I've never even met the prince. And why do you care if he'll listen to me?"

"Because you have the mind of a scholar in the body of a lord," she said. "A rare and precious combination in this dark age. These traits make you worthy to protect the sacred knowledge—that which the empire must preserve if the world shall live. I have not foreseen another like you in all of Francia, but the choice remains yours." She turned to walk away. "Angelica will tend to your wounds. If you choose to learn more, return here before All Hallows Eve."

I stared in disbelief as Orionde departed, followed by her warriors. She had manipulated all of this. The deaths of my father and my brother, for what? So I could become a counselor to a man who was not even king. All to protect some mysterious sacred knowledge. My mind ached. None of this made sense. Then I felt a big velvety nose against my cheek. Bayard nudged my head toward Angelica.

She gave me a sympathetic smile. "May I?"

I nodded yes, for again, I had nothing to lose. The sickness that thinned my blood was sure to kill me without her aid, and this time I had no desire to push her away. "This won't hurt," she said, kneeling by my side. She cupped the crystal in her hand and blew on it, whispering the same strange word she had before. Light exploded within the crystal, as brilliant as any I had ever beheld.

"She taught you this?" I asked.

"She taught me everything. And she'll teach you too if you let her." She pressed the crystal to my wounded thigh and uttered a foreign verse with the melody of a song. While the warmth of the crystal's

78

light bathed my leg, I watched in awe as she kneaded the torn flesh back together with her free hand, the way a potter molds a vessel from clay. As she continued to speak the alien words, her fingers worked my flesh into a scar across my thigh, sealing my cut. Muscles that only moments before throbbed with pain, now felt warm and healthy.

Next, she helped me remove my mail hauberk and went to work on my shoulder. The wound was not nearly as bad as my thigh, but blood covered my skin all the way to my elbow. As I felt her words and her light healing the wound, a thought struck. With this power—whatever it might be—I'd never risk bleeding to death again. Never in my life had I imagined such a future. The notion added fuel to the torrent of thoughts burning in my mind.

"So the whole time you were at Aygremont," I asked, "you were doing her bidding?"

"The entire time."

"Yet you slept with Vivian." I cringed at the thought of what the two of them had done within his chamber.

"It helped you escape, didn't it? I was the one who warned Odo that your life was in danger, and I made sure Vivian was too preoccupied to do the deed himself."

Odo had been warned. Suddenly, his surprise upon seeing Angelica on the battlefield started to make sense.

"Also," she continued, "what better way was there to learn Vivian's intentions? It's the whole reason I knew he'd send his army to meet you in the Val d'Anglin. I sent a messenger to Limoges to make sure you learned that too."

I rubbed my forehead; a troubling thought still gnawed at my brain. "But you shared his bed?"

She ran her hand behind my neck, and I'll admit, I welcomed her touch. "It was all in the call of duty," she said. "I swear it."

I gazed at Angelica. She was beautiful, too, but in a seemingly mortal sense, unlike Orionde. Even so, I had to know the truth. "Are you one of them?"

"No." She shook her head. "I'm as human as you are."

"And they're truly of the Fae?"

"You can call them that," she said, "but if you stick around, you'll find the truth is a good bit different from the legends."

I let that thought sink in. What else could they be? And why were they so concerned about the affairs of men? "This talk about Charles and an empire—do you believe it?"

"Orionde can sometimes see the future. She knows of what she speaks. If you return here before All Hallows Eve, you'll find out more."

My head fell into my hands. Never had I felt so overwhelmed. I looked back at the place where I had killed my brother. His body was still lying on the barren plain. "What do I do now?"

Angelica glanced at Vivian without a hint of remorse in her eyes. "Bury him next to your father, but before then, let all of Aygremont know who their rightful lord is. You can take Bayard for now. I even think he likes you. If you choose not to return, he can find his way back."

I nodded slowly. I couldn't leave Vivian in this place, even though he had tried to kill me. Besides, the thought of returning to the Val d'Anglin reminded me of Renaud, and Guichard, and Odo, too. I had to know whether they survived. I patted Bayard on the neck. He responded with a loud snort. I welcomed the stallion's companionship, but one thing seemed clear: Angelica was not coming with me.

"If I return," I asked, "how will I find my way through the forest and the mists?" I eyed the impossibly tall tower that looked as if it had been carved from a titanic piece of reddish stone, similar to the hard surface of this otherwise desolate plain. "What do you even call this place?"

"You're at the tower of Rosefleur." Angelica lifted her chin. "And if you return, she will know of your coming—and I promise, I'll be there at the forest's edge to greet you."

WITH VIVIAN'S BODY DRAPED OVER THE STALLION'S LOWER BACK, I RODE Bayard to the forest's edge as dusk fell upon the Val d'Anglin. I entered the field from the shadows beneath the gnarled and overgrown trees —where thirty archers stood to greet me. Bows drawn, they aimed their arrows at my chest.

My stomach clenched. Behind the row of archers, a mail-clad horseman called out a warning. "Vivian, we've crushed your army. Surrender now, or die!"

Vivian? It took me a moment to recognize Renaud's voice. In the distance, beside a cluster of horsemen, I spied a crimson banner, and I knew it bore an image of the three crowned lions of Dordogne. I couldn't fathom how Renaud had prevailed after that disastrous charge, but somehow he had. I slowly raised my hands, a smile spreading across my face.

"Vivian," Renaud hollered, "there's no need to shed more blood today."

"Agreed," I answered. "Too much blood's been shed."

Renaud cocked his head. "Maugis?"

"You were expecting someone else," I admitted.

"Maugis!" Renaud beamed. "Stand down, men. By God's grace, the rightful lord of Aygremont has returned!" Renaud spurred his charger forward.

Guichard rode behind him. "Cousin," he exclaimed, "you're alive!"

They slowed their mounts as they reached me, their expressions filled with elation. Renaud glanced at my brother's battered body. "Is that Vivian?"

"He was driven mad with rage," I explained. "He would have killed me if it weren't for Bayard here." I patted the stallion's neck.

"That's one monstrous beast," Guichard said. Bayard responded by baring his teeth and stomping one of his massive hooves.

I smiled weakly. "Believe it or not, he understands what you're saying. He's terribly intelligent. I wouldn't make him angry."

Guichard gave the stallion a wary look. "Honestly?"

"As true as the sun rises in the east," I replied. Guichard urged his charger back a step.

I gestured toward the assembled archers. "How did you do it?"

"It was all thanks to you," Renaud explained. "After our retreat, I heard you fled into the forest. Vivian and the Lion took their best captains and went in after you, along with all of their war hounds. I haven't seen one of them come out of there yet."

I felt a cold shiver as I recalled the men dying in the boneyard at the hands of the undead.

"The men they left behind," Guichard added, "weren't the sharpest swords in the armory. Which reminds me, Maugis. When you return to Aygremont, put improving education high on your agenda."

"Guichard's right, you know," Renaud continued. "The mind is a terrible thing to waste. Anyhow, the men that remained never figured we'd rally our troops and lead a second attack. Most of them surrendered, but I'm sure a lot of them are holding out hope that Vivian will return to save the day. I suspect they'll be of a new mind once they learn of his fate."

Renaud looked me over. "You look relatively unscathed. Did Vivian even land a cut on you?"

"That's a long story," I said, but talk of wounds turned my thoughts to another old friend. "What about Odo? The Lion shot him twice."

"He'll live," Guichard replied, "but the arrows have made him as cantankerous as the devil."

My spirits surged at the news. "Where is he?"

After leaving Bayard and Vivian with Renaud and his archers, Guichard led me to their camp where the banners of Dordogne and Limoges flew proudly. Around clusters of tents, battle-weary men huddled over campfires. Some supped on bread and ale, while others sat or lay on the ground as healers tended to their wounds, bandaging cuts and splinting broken limbs. The men who fought for Vivian sat on a field encircled by two-dozen of Renaud's warriors, while a group of tents on the other side of the encampment formed a makeshift infirmary for the most injured men. There, we found Odo. Thick bandages wrapped his shoulder and ribs as he drank from a swollen aleskin. When he saw me enter the tent, he nearly spit out a mouthful of ale. "Maugis!"

I could not contain my grin. "Thank the saints you're alive!"

"That piss-bastard of a huntsman tried his best," Odo said, "but it turns out I'm a hard man to kill. But what about you? The last I saw, Angelica took you into the forest. She was the one that warned me the night we fled Aygremont. I never expected to see her here."

"I'm afraid there's more to her than meets the eye. She saved me from the battlefield, but Vivian still found me."

Odo raised an eyebrow. "Yet you're here, and he's not."

I drew in a long breath. "Let's just say, there's only one lord of Aygremont now. And he's going to need a good steward."

Odo shook his head. "For heaven's sake, lad. How on God's good Earth did you beat him?"

"Just like you told me to," I said. "I used my wits."

16

THE ESSENCE OF EVIL

I suppose that could have been the end of the story. After all, I became the sole lord of Aygremont, Odo survived his wounds, and Renaud won the battle, earning fame throughout Francia. I swore to become a just ruler, the likes of which the people of Aygremont had not seen in generations. I opened the forest so that anyone could hunt there to provide food for their families. At harvest time, I threw a grand festival to celebrate the new way of life in Aygremont. I even followed Guichard's advice and founded a school. But that would not have answered your questions about how I came to know Orionde, would it? No, there is more to tell—and it's the reason a demon just chased us down the Seine.

Still, it starts back at Aygremont. After my return, no matter how hard I tried, I could not take my mind off Angelica, and Rosefleur, and Orionde's parting words. *If you choose to learn more, return here before All Hallows Eve...*

How could I ever forget what I had seen? I had discovered a place the storytellers only dreamed of. The land of faerie. The place the Celts called the Otherworld. It was not some gloomy Sheol where the spirits of the dead lingered in sorrow, as some myths held, but the realm of Rosefleur, that magnificent spire which contained such knowledge inside its stone-hewn walls. All the warnings Grand-mother and Odo ever gave me about the Fae seemed but ghost stories now. Angelica lived safely among the Fae women, and Orionde did not strike me as some seductress bent on stealing my spirit from its mortal shell. Instead, she offered knowledge—a sacred truth of the kind I'd longed for since my youth. An understanding that few men were privileged to possess. How could I resist that allure?

A week before All Hallows Eve, I put Odo in charge of Aygremont and promised to return from my sabbatical by the next harvest. Days later, I donned my mail hauberk, strapped a new sword at my side, and rode Bayard to the Val d'Anglin until we reached the forest.

And at the forest edge, Angelica stood there to greet us.

She wore a close-fitting, white gown similar to the one Orionde had worn on the day when I fought Vivian, with a white cloak trimmed with fox fur. Her raven hair fell over her shoulders, and she looked up with a warm smile. I had never seen her look so beautiful. When I dismounted Bayard, she embraced me. Her skin was soft against my own, and I caught the scent of her hair. When she brushed a kiss on my cheek, I wondered if I would ever want to leave this place.

I took Bayard's reins and followed Angelica on foot through the forest. It's hard to describe how beautiful the forest was when there weren't men racing through it trying to kill you. The woods felt wondrously primeval, with oaks hundreds of years old, their trunks clothed with green moss. From their branches, hanging moss swayed like ribbons, and toadstools of every shape and color sprouted between the ancient tree roots. And amidst the trees, the forest was alive with creatures of a kind I had never seen before: Martins and minks with fur that shone like gold scurrying across the boughs, deer as white as snow browsing in the glades, and a silver-haired lynx stalking squirrels from the tree limbs.

After trudging deep into the forest, we reached the strange curtain of mist that perpetually hung like a barrier between the trees, but the vapor looked thinner than before. "What is this mist?" I asked Angelica.

"It's the border between this world and the Otherworld," she said.

"It was thicker the last time we were here. Why is the barrier so thin now?"

"Because tomorrow is All Hallows Eve," she replied. "On that night, the curtain that separates the Otherworld begins to fray. But even then, a person could not find their way to Rosefleur without the proper tools." She pulled the hazel-nut-sized crystal from a pocket in her cloak and held it close to her lips. Then she closed her eyes and whispered the word I had heard her say before. *Eoh.* Her soul light flared within the crystal. When the light settled into a glow, Angelica reached her hand into the curtain, and the mists began to part as if her light had caused a stiff breeze to separate the vapor. Taking my hand, she led Bayard and me through the mist-filled portion of the forest that I had known as the boneyard. The scores of skeletons were still there, covered in moss as if the woods were reclaiming the bones. I suspected Vivian's men lay among them.

"All these men," I asked, "how did they die?"

Her gaze wandered to the overgrown corpses. "They didn't have the light. It's a dreadful idea to enter the Otherworld when you don't know what you're doing."

"Then how did I get through the mists without the light?"

"Because Orionde created a pathway for you to escape," she explained. "The barrier bends to her will. But without her, you would have wandered there, lost within the mists for days until you starved to death and ended up like them." She put a hand on my cheek and grinned. "I'm happy you didn't end up a corpse."

Her touch sent a tingle down my neck, and I felt right then that I would follow this woman anywhere. Eventually, she led us from the boneyard to the barren plain of reddish stone where the towering spire of Rosefleur soared into a platinum sky.

Much happened after the day I set foot inside the tower. Suffice it to say, we found Orionde, and I met the Fae women who lived with her. They called themselves the Sisters of Orionde, and over time I learned more about their nature. They were refugees, you see, from the war that broke out in Heaven. The one the priests preach about from Scripture. To call them angels would be a mistake, for paradise is forever denied them, but perhaps, when the world was born, that may have been an apt description. The Fae taught me everything I know about the powers I can wield, derived from a language as old as creation. But the tale of my apprenticeship will have to wait for another day. Rather, it is the events on All Hallows Eve, the night after I arrived at Rosefleur, that matter most to this story.

That night, Angelica and I met Orionde in the tower's vestibule. She stood in its center like a white-clad goddess aglow in light flickering from fires that burned in braziers set into the walls of the circular chamber. A book satchel was slung over her shoulder. "You made the choice I hoped you would," she said. "Allow me to show you why I need your aid." She beckoned me to follow her.

I glanced at Angelica, who gave a slight nod, but she did not join us as I followed Orionde through one of the vestibule's towering archways. The archway led to a stairwell. When Orionde started down the curved flight of stairs, smaller braziers set into the walls flicked alight as if her mere presence brought them to life. Descending each step, I began to imagine the secrets Orionde could teach me—and how much everything had just changed. My entire world, which for years had been isolated to the lands of Dordogne and dreams of Aygremont, suddenly seemed as vast as an ocean, and the promise of what I might learn stretched beyond the horizon.

The stairwell continued for what must have been a hundred feet or more beneath the tower, ending in a small cavern. The air inside was damp and cold. A stream of luminescent water trickled down a fissure in the rock wall and gathered into a natural pool. Like the stream, the pool glowed with the color of moonlight, illuminating the area. "The scrying pool of Rosefleur is a window into the past where the darkest secrets are hidden. Secrets that mankind has since forgotten."

She set down the satchel and knelt before the scrying pool, urging me to join her. Then she took my hand in hers. Unlike the soft warmth of Angelica's skin, Orionde's touch was as hard and cold as stone. "You will need my aid to see into the pool." With the fingers of her free hand, she stirred up the waters. As they swirled, the glowing

JOSEPH FINLEY

light formed into shapes, and as they transformed into images, I found my consciousness being drawn toward the pool.

"Do not fight the sensation," Orionde said. "Let your mind see through the window."

I exhaled and thought of nothing but the pool. Where before I saw swirling water, I now saw flames within the pool. Behind those flames slithered something long and serpentine. Its scales glowed like embers, its eyes blazed like the sun, and fire spilled from its mouth. I wanted to pull away, for, in all my life, I had never witnessed a creature so terrifying, but Orionde held my hand tight, her grip as hard as steel.

"Long before men recorded the passage of time," she began, "there was the Dragon. For an age, he ruled the world of men until the Earth cracked, and the floodwaters came and brought ruin to mankind. He was imprisoned in the Underworld, but still, his influence spread from the cavernous darkness into the mortal world, where his servants awaited his return. The ancients remembered him, the Babylonians, the Arabs, the Hebrews, the Greeks. They called him by many names— Ophion, Huwawa, Samyaza, Lucifer, and Shaitan. Their stories of him became myths, and those myths became legends, many of which have long been forgotten. Yet throughout history, there have been times when the Dragon has roamed free of his prison. And in those moments, however brief, the fate of humanity has hung in the balance."

The image of the dragon began to fade, but the flames remained, and engulfed within them, I saw a city with soaring towers. As the fire burned, the earth quaked, and the towers collapsed in torrents of rubble that washed into the sea. "Kingdoms fell to ruin," she said. "Thousands were slaughtered, and the air filled with the souls of the dead." The ruined city faded into the image of a battlefield. Spears and arrows jutted from hundreds of corpses, and across the battlefield moved the shadow of an enormous flying beast. From the dead bodies rose motes of light like sparks from a bonfire wafting into the night. The image of the battlefield dissolved, and the sparks settled into stars as if I were gazing upon a clear night sky.

"So it is written, in the oldest of prophecies, etched within the heavens. The prophecy warns of the Dragon's return and the great war he will wage. Yet the prophecy also speaks of a weapon that can defeat him."

Before my eyes, one of the stars fell from the sky. I followed its rapid descent until it plummeted into a snow-filled plain, the force of its impact blasting a crater into the Earth. Amid the snow, the object glowed as pure and white as the North Star at midnight.

"The Atlanteans," Orionde continued, "discovered the Stone of Light in the first age at the ends of the whole Earth, as foretold by the words of the prophet Enoch. Three times the weapon has defeated the Dragon and driven him back to the Underworld. But the day is coming when it will be needed again. Already, the Dragon's servants are searching for it, and if they find it, all will be lost."

The object's light dimmed. The snow melted into flames, and once again, I saw the Dragon's burning scales, and with it, I saw demons clawing through the fire. Hatred burned in their eyes as they scrabbled like rats from the flames before the Dragon opened his mouth and let out a roar that shook the ground beneath my knees. My blood ran cold, and a scream gathered in my throat—but Orionde pulled me back. In a breath, I was staring at the luminescent water of the pool. The Dragon and its demons were gone.

She stood and helped me to my feet. "Since the beginning of this millennium," she said, "the bishops of Rome had preserved the secrets of the prophecy and the weapon. When Constantine became emperor, the might of the Roman Empire helped protect those secrets from the Dragon's servants. Though when the Roman Empire fell, those secrets were scattered like torn parchment into the wind, as was so much of the Romans' knowledge that has been lost now from the world of men.

"Yet through the scrying pool, I have foreseen that a new Roman Empire shall be born, and Prince Charles shall be the blacksmith to forge it together. Though if this new empire is to protect the secrets as the old one did in the time of Constantine, you must lead that cause from within. As Charles's peer and his advisor—as one of his paladins. That is why I have chosen you."

I still did not understand why she found me worthy of her trust, but how could I refuse her, after everything I had seen in the scrying pool? I had felt the Dragon's presence as if it been within the cavern, and never before had I beheld something so terrifying. This was a threat far beyond the machinations of tyrant lords or the Moorish hordes in Spain. For as certain as I was of anything in my life, I had gazed upon the essence of evil. The Dragon of Revelation. The enemy of God. What greater cause could a man devote his life to than the defeat of evil incarnate?

Orionde removed a book from the satchel. A metal clasp kept the book closed, preventing the mass of vellum pages from bursting open. Lacework patterns were embossed on its dark leather cover, and a prominent symbol dominated its center dusted in gold: a *crux ansata*— a cross with a looped head. It was a hieroglyph that I would come to know as an ankh—an ancient symbol of life.

"You have seen but a glimpse of the truth," Orionde said. "For the great task that lies ahead, I will arm you with knowledge beyond your imagination, and you will fill this book's pages with the secrets I teach you. All you must do is answer the call."

I knew what she wanted, and knew I was ready. I held out my hands, and she gave me the book.

And that is how I came to know Orionde le Fae.

III

AFTERMATH

WHAT FOLLOWS FEAR?

Inside the refectory, the snap of an ember from the hearth broke the silence after Maugis finished his tale. Turpin gazed reflectively, having ignored his half-empty cup of wine. The archbishop had heard the story of the scrying pool before, but its gravity was not lost on him this second time. Beside him, Roland glanced down and sighed. While across the table, Bradamante looked Maugis in the eyes. "So that's how you met her?" she asked, her expression hardening before him.

"Orionde?" Maugis replied, puzzled by her reaction. "That's how I met her. It's the whole point of the story."

With a faint grimace, Roland set down his cup. "She means Angelica."

"Ahh…" Maugis glanced away. "Right." How could any of them forget the trouble Angelica ended up causing? And Bradamante had a particular reason to hate her, for just four years ago, Angelica almost cost Roland his life. When his apprenticeship began, Maugis never would have imagined that Angelica would pose a greater threat to the paladins than any of Charles's enemies.

"I couldn't tell the tale without mentioning her," Maugis confessed.

"She was a different person back then. We both were. Sometimes, people change for the worse."

"That they do," Turpin interjected. "But she wasn't the point of the story. Maugis has witnessed the enemy we're facing. And if that demon's not proof of it, I don't know what is. Those things Orionde showed him in that pool, it's the whole reason we're on this bloody quest—to retrieve the Stone and protect it."

Roland looked up. "Turpin's right. What Angelica did is in the past. She's not our concern anymore."

"Still," Bradamante said, "I'll never forgive her for what she did."

"She doesn't need your forgiveness," Turpin reminded her. "Angelica's dead. She answers to God now."

Maugis felt a pang of sorrow in his chest. Angelica had been his first love, and he still found it hard to imagine how an affair that began with so much happiness and light could turn so suddenly dark. At least it had seemed sudden back then, a year after his apprenticeship with Orionde had begun. He was still naive in those early days and had failed to see the warning signs. By the time she betrayed him —betrayed *all* of them—he had thought he had hated the person she had become. But that, too, was a lie, and the pain of losing her still stung like the cut of a jagged knife.

His thoughts turned from Angelica when a whiff of smoke burned his nostrils. He glanced around the room. The smell was not coming from the hearth, but his eyes flew wide when he saw smoke curling through the gaps in the shuttered windows.

Roland noticed it, too. "Something's burning!"

"The door!" Turpin yelled. From beneath the doorsill seeped tendrils of black smoke. More smoke hissed through the side jams.

Bradamante gasped. "The building's on fire!"

From outside came the cries of men. Billows of smoke began to gather in the refectory's rafters. From the hot orange glow surrounding them, Maugis suspected the roof was aflame too. "We have to get out of here now!"

Roland rushed to the door and tried to rip it open, but the door did not budge. "It's locked!"

"Why would the monks lock us in the refectory?" Bradamante asked, panic rising in her voice.

Turpin covered his mouth with his arm. "I fear it wasn't the monks."

The archbishop's suggestion sent a stab of concern through Maugis, but now was no time to worry about what had caused the fire. Smoke was flooding through the cracks in the shutters and around the door. A sea of black vapor filled the refectory's ceiling, and tongues of flame licked the walls below the roof. A loud crack sounded from the rafters, followed by a burst of sparks.

With a roar, Roland threw his shoulder into the burning door. The door's oak planks barely moved. "What sorcery is this!" Roland rasped.

Turpin coughed. "The hellborn kind!"

Maugis grimaced. The mythology Turpin had recounted about Phobos should have warned them, but now it might be too late.

Flames engulfed the shutters over the windows. "What do you mean?" Bradamante asked, hacking from the smoke.

"That there was more than one demon in that storm!" Turpin growled.

Bradamante gazed back in horror, but Maugis had already reached the same conclusion. The smoke was burning his eyes, and he knew they only had precious moments before the fire would overwhelm them. "Grab whatever you can carry," he cried, "and someone save that casket!"

From the pile of his own belongings, Maugis snatched the satchel and slung it over his shoulder. Then he lifted his blackened staff. *Staff kindles fire*, Maugis thought, *and binds flames*. Ignoring the fumes burning his throat, he cleared his mind and spoke the ancient words Orionde had taught him years ago at Rosefleur. With each syllable, the air thrummed, and a faint blue light flickered from the staff. Heat surged through Maugis' arms as the staff, imbued with the power of his words, summoned the flames.

With a shuddering boom, fire burst through the shutters and roared toward the staff. From beneath the doorsill and the burning roof, more flames rushed toward him, gathering around the tip of his staff like a blazing storm. Flames singed Maugis' cheek, and he knew he could not contain the fire for more than a few breaths.

As soon as he saw his friends were clear, he released his hold on the fire and focused all his will on the door. A torrent of flames surged from the staff to the door, striking the oak boards like a bolt of lightning. The door exploded with a sound like thunder. Burning wooden planks and shards blasted in every direction, leaving only the blackened frame where the door had been.

"Now, run!" Maugis yelled.

With his flanged mace in one hand and the casket in another, Turpin ducked through the charred doorframe. Bradamante followed him, clutching her mail coat and her sword. Roland pointed Durendal at the doorway. "Go!"

Maugis darted through the doorway into the cloister, only to find himself surrounded by an inferno. Fire burned from every building in the abbey. Frantic monks scrambled from the dormitory, which was engulfed in flames, while the hungry blaze consumed the wooden roof above the cloister's walkways. A smoky haze filled the garden in the center of the cloister, and within it stood the gatekeeper. Bathed in the fire's hellish glow, his youthful face contorted with a mix of rage and madness. He raised his arms above his head, and with each gesture of his long-fingered hands, flames flared from the burning structures. "My breath is like brimstone!" the gatekeeper raved. "Let this abbey be kindling to my sacred flames!"

"Christ," Roland swore as he joined them in the cloister.

Maugis mustered his courage, trying to ignore the weariness in his bones that followed such a rigorous use of the power. Bradamante and Turpin crouched in a defensive stance, their weapons raised toward the gatekeeper. "It must have possessed him when he left the abbey to save the fisherman," Turpin said under his breath.

The gatekeeper leered at the paladins. "Fire shall fall upon you, and the dead shall follow!"

He swept his arms downward. The beams supporting the cloister's shingled roof cracked, and with a shower of glowing sparks, gave way.

Maugis' breath caught in his throat, and the roof crashed down like a rain of fire.

THE FACE OF TERROR

As the cloister's roof collapsed around them, Roland pulled Maugis under his shield, blocking the hunks of burning wood. Falling sparks singed Maugis' skin, but Roland's shield had saved them from any bone-crushing debris.

With a roar, Turpin heaved away a large piece of the roof. Soot and sweat streaked down his face, while Bradamante crouched safely beneath his broad chest. Roland pulled Maugis into the cloister's garden, but heat flared up Maugis' neck. "Your cloak's on fire," Roland yelled.

Maugis ripped off his brooch and shed his burning cloak, wincing from his burns. He checked his sleeves and breeches, but neither had succumbed to the flames. Then he glanced around the garden. The gatekeeper was gone.

"Where did he go?" Bradamante asked, gripping her sword as if she was itching to use it.

"The only way he could have," Turpin growled. He pointed to a haze-filled archway at the far end of the only walkway with part of its roof still intact.

"When we find him," Roland said, between huffs of breath, "one blow from Durendal will send him back to hell."

Maugis shook his head. "You can't kill the gatekeeper. He's an innocent man, just possessed."

Roland's lips curled into a snarl. "Whatever he is, he will burn down the entire abbey. How many lives will that cost?"

"We're wasting time," Bradamante insisted, throwing aside her mail coat. "You can debate killing him when we catch him." She bolted for the archway.

The three men ran after her, ducking beneath the arch and emerging onto a field behind the church. Flames belched from windows in the choir, billowing plumes of smoke high above the abbey. The haze blotted out the stars above. A gaggle of terrified monks stood by, transfixed on the blaze. The abbot was among them, shaking and praying.

"Where's the gatekeeper?" Maugis demanded.

The abbot looked at him, his face white with fear. "Lay Brother Hugo? He's lost his mind!"

"He's been possessed," Maugis explained. "An evil spirit guides his actions."

"I saw him," volunteered one of the monks. "He ran toward the graveyard."

Maugis swore under his breath. "Bloody hell!"

Turpin shot him a concerned look. "May the dead follow. That was his warning."

"Which is what I'm afraid of." Maugis glanced where the monk was pointing. At the end of the field rose a hillock awash in the fog of smoke. He could see the outline of gravestones atop the hill, but among them were other shapes, manlike in form. And they were moving.

Maugis' thoughts flashed to a memory of the boneyard surrounding Rosefleur and the cries of Vivian's men being ravaged by the dead. Orionde had never taught him the necromancy she used eleven years ago, for those were dark arts no man was meant to know. But the sick feeling in his gut told him a demon would be a master of those arts.

Roland peered up the hillock. "What in the hell is moving up there?"

Maugis sighed. "How many men are buried in that graveyard?" he asked the monks.

"We lost twenty to the plague just last winter," the abbot said, cringing. "But this abbey is more than a hundred years old. There would be scores upon scores."

"That's the answer to your question," he told Roland.

"Sweet Mother of Mercy," Turpin muttered.

Bradamante shook her head. "Can the dead be killed?"

"We're about to find out," Roland said, his jaw set.

Turpin handed Maugis the casket. "You'll need this."

With a nod, Maugis took the casket and cradled it in his left arm. "Just keep them off me."

"Stay close," Roland told his companions. "We'll form a wedge in front of Maugis. I'll be the tip of the spear."

Maugis' pulse quickened as they strode toward the hillock. When they started up the slope, the stench of rot and decay overwhelmed the scent of burning wood. Maugis fought off a sense of nausea brought on by the foul odor, then Bradamante gasped as the enemy shambled from among the gravestones. Skeletal in form and caked in the dirt from which they had crawled, some had remnants of muscles and flesh; others wore the worm-eaten remains of Benedictine habits with ribcages showing through the holes between the rotting wool. Many had skulls of yellow bone with sockets black as the night, while a few stared back with milky eyes that had not yet melted away in death. The undead vanguard numbered over two dozen, and a chilling sound hissed from their lungless chests.

From behind the wall of living dead, raved the gatekeeper. "Let the dead be the plague that strikes down our enemies and brings ruin upon them!"

Roland gripped his shield and sword. "Let's go kill the dead—for God and King Charles!"

He charged the nearest pair of corpses, smashing the first with the boss of his shield and cleaving the second one's skull from its neck. Bradamante struck as quickly as her cousin, slashing through bone and dead flesh, while Turpin hammered his mace, crushing the first skull it met. The undead surged toward the paladins like the rats from the courtyard, clawing with their boney talons and biting with their earth-stained teeth. Durendal scythed through another pair, but as soon as one fell, a third was there to take its place. Maugis knew that their sheer number would soon overtake his friends.

He tried to clear his mind to invoke the power, but one of the corpses peeled off from Turpin and clambered toward him. Pinholes of fire burned where its eyes had been. With all his strength, Maugis slammed his blackened staff into the thing's head. The impact knocked the skull from its shoulders, but even headless, the creature lunged. Broken nails tore through Maugis' tunic and into his flesh. He cried out in pain, just as Turpin spun around with a blow that shattered the creature's spine. Another corpse leaped onto Turpin's back and wrapped its boney finger's around the archbishop's neck.

"Do it," Turpin gagged, as two more of the undead tried to wrestle the mace from his hands.

Maugis drew in a deep breath, trying to calm his drumming heart. His mind settled on the words, and he felt a crackle of power in his lungs. "Demon!" he cried to get its attention.

The gatekeeper rose above the backs of the voracious mob of corpses, waving his arms to beckon them forward. His eyes flared with primal rage. "My army shall devour you all!"

Maugis tossed aside his staff and took the casket with both hands. "I learned a long time ago it's not the size of a man's army that makes him strong, but his wits!" He spoke three words to stun the demon already trapped within the casket long enough to prevent its escape, and then let another verse roll off his tongue. The surrounding air began to sizzle. The gatekeeper's eyes flew wide as the demon inside him realized what was happening.

"Kill him!" the gatekeeper screamed.

On his command, the undead horde trained their gaze on Maugis, but by then it was too late. Maugis cracked the lid open and uttered the true name of the demon who had possessed the gatekeeper. *"Deimos!"*

A bluish fire filled the gatekeeper's gaping mouth. His body convulsed, and with a horrid wail, the fire streamed from his jaws in a flaming arc toward the casket. Wisps of azure flames filled the vessel, and when the whole of the demon's essence was inside it, a blast of wind exploded around the gatekeeper. The gale nearly knocked Maugis off his feet, but he fought to maintain his balance, clutching the casket with all of his remaining strength.

In the silence that followed, the undead horde stopped and stared at Maugis. The mass of corpses began to sway like a tavern drunk who had imbibed too much ale. Then, in unison, their knees buckled, and the army of the dead crashed to the ground.

THE CALM AFTER THE STORM

Maugis stumbled down the hill, away from the stench of the graveyard, and fell to a knee. A wave of exhaustion washed through his muscles. Wielding the power always took a physical toll, and after controlling the fire and trapping the demon, he did not know when he might have the strength to stand again. He set down the casket. Something rattled inside, followed by a duo of faint, yet desperate moans.

Turpin slumped to the ground beside Maugis, trying to catch his breath after the undead had nearly choked it from his lungs. "Thank God and good Saint Denis," he said with a cough. "You got the foul bastard."

Bradamante groaned as she sat down next to them. Blood and dirt stained her cheek and a bare shoulder peeked through her shredded tunic. She glanced back, watching Roland drag the gatekeeper's body from the graveyard. "Don't worry," Roland said with a faint smile, "I didn't kill him. He's unconscious, but still breathing."

Maugis gave a grateful nod.

After laying down the gatekeeper, Roland stabbed Durendal into the ground and joined them. He turned to Maugis. "I'm glad you chose not to keep this sword."

"It always suited you better," Maugis said. "Besides, it was too heavy for my tastes."

Roland smiled. "That magic, or whatever you call it, suits you just fine. We wouldn't have lasted long if you hadn't captured that thing."

"I couldn't have done it without you," Maugis said. "All of you."

Bradamante put her hand on Maugis' shoulder. "None of us could have done what you did."

"And it's a good thing you remembered your mythology," Turpin added.

"Phobos and Deimos," Maugis replied. "Fear and terror. When we encountered one, we should have known his brother would not be far behind."

"There's no chance they were triplets?" Roland quipped.

Maugis laughed. "In the myths, Aphrodite and Ares only had the two little devils."

"How did they enter hallowed ground?" Bradamante asked.

"That one's a mystery," Turpin said, "though I have a theory. Perhaps once they possess a human form, they can go anywhere a human could? As if the mortal shell surrounding their condemned spirits works as a barrier of sorts against the holiness of this ground."

"I was thinking the same thing," Maugis admitted. "But the more crucial question, however, is *who* sent these demons against us? Whoever hired those men to accost me in Paris, called himself the Blackbird. I have to believe that he's the sorcerer who sent them after us."

Turpin scratched his beard. "He knew of your mission too. He must be a member of the palace."

"Orionde suspected there was a spy in the King's court," Maugis reminded them.

"But who?" Roland ran his fingers through his hair. "The twelve are loyal to Charles, and we've known these men for years."

"Unless the spy's not man," Bradamante pointed out. "How many ladies—and mistresses—are lurking about the palace?"

Her words made Maugis think of Angelica. She was the one

person he knew capable of summoning the things they had just defeated. But it could not have been her. She was gone.

A loud crash snapped his thoughts back to the present. Across the field, the steeple of the church collapsed in fiery ruin into the blaze claiming the abbey.

Bradamante clasped her hands together. "There's no saving it."

"No," Turpin said, "but they'll rebuild. Monks are heartier souls than most realize. Evil may have come to this abbey, but it won't stop them. The brotherhood will press on."

Maugis set his jaw. "And so shall we."

"We'll need a new boat," Roland pointed out. "Unless we're going to swim across the channel."

"I was never a good swimmer," Maugis admitted, his lips curling into a smile. "I tend to sink."

Bradamante cocked her head. "Is this your attempt at graveyard humor?"

"It's always good to laugh in the face of death," Turpin replied with a grin.

"Though it helps when you can stab death with a sword," Roland remarked.

"True," Bradamante said. "At least this trouble won't be following us to Britannia."

Maugis glanced down. If what Orionde had told him was true, a far greater danger than two demons awaited them in Britannia. But this was no time to darken his friends' moods. He looked up at them. "We still have a long journey ahead. But I'm grateful you three are at my side."

"Three lords and a warrior fair," Turpin said. "We make a fine team."

Bradamante gave Maugis a smile. "And we wouldn't have it any other way."

HISTORICAL NOTE

This prequel recounts the first leg of a journey referenced in both *Enoch's Device* and *The Key to the Abyss*. But the central part of the story, *Maugis' Tale*, is a reimagining of the medieval poem titled *Maugis d'Aygremont et de Vivian son Frère* ("Maugis of Aygremont and Vivian his Brother"). The story was one of many epic poems, known as *chansons de geste* ("songs of deeds"), composed in France beginning around the 12th century.

In the original *chanson de geste*, Maugis, the son of Count Bevis and the twin brother of Vivian, is kidnapped as an infant by one of Bevis's household servants. After escaping the castle, the servant lays down to rest in a forest, where she and the infant are attacked by a lion and a leopard. After killing the servant, the great cats kill one another while fighting over the child. Maugis is eventually rescued by Orionde the Fae, who takes the infant to her home at Rosefleur. There, she and her sister Fae raise Maugis to manhood and teach him the magical arts. Soon after, Maugis encounters the enchanted horse, Bayard, and even engages in a battle with his brother, Vivian, who, according to the poem, was also kidnaped as a child and raised in the court of a Moorish king. In another *chanson de gest*, Maugis becomes one of the twelve paladins of Charlemagne. Although in those stories, he remains more of a Merlin-like enchanter than a belted knight.

Because an infant hardly makes for a compelling protagonist, I chose to make Maugis nineteen and replace the actual lion and leopard with the symbolic characters of the Lion and Vivian (giving the House of Aygremont the leopard as its heraldic symbol). The character of Orionde, who plays a significant role in *Enoch's Device*, came straight from the medieval epic poem, as did Rosefleur and Orionde's sister Fae. I've always loved stories that reimagine fairy tales and legends, and Maugis d'Aygremont offered me a chance to try my hand at one.

Many other characters in the story were also made famous in medieval literature. Renaud and his brothers are the heroes of their own *chansons de gest*, and their adventures include their cousin Maugis and his mighty steed, Bayard. In time, both Maugis and Renaud come to serve Charlemagne. And in the epic poems about the paladins, Angelica features prominently.

In those stories, she is a princess of Cathay (a medieval European name for China), but those poems were composed after the time of Marco Polo, when the Far East was more front of mind. It is hard to believe that many 8th-century Franks would have encountered an Asian princess, so I took it upon myself to give Angelica a more realistic origin.

Bradamante, Roland, and Turpin are also major characters in the *chansons de gest* about the paladins of Charlemagne. These stories, known collectively as *The Matter of France*, became the subject of several famous Renaissance poems, including *Orlando Innamorato* and *Orlando Furioso*. Two of these three legendary characters, however, were based on real historical figures. Roland was a Frankish count who served Charlemagne as prefect of the Breton March. By most accounts, he fought and died in 778 at the Battle of Roncesvalles Pass, which is the subject of another epic poem titled *The Song of Roland*. In the years following *The Song of Roland*, Roland would become known as a hero, a martyr, and the epitome of a virtuous Christian knight. His sword, Durendal, may be the most legendary blade next to King

Arthur's Excalibur. And, for fans of fantasy fiction, Roland became the inspiration for Roland Deschain, the hero of Stephen King's *The Dark Tower* series.

Turpin served as Archbishop of Reims from around the year 748 until his death in the year 794, though some accounts have him living until the year 800. Also, his real name may have been Tilpin. He began his career as a monk at Saint-Denis in Paris and, as archbishop, may have presided over the funeral of Charlemagne's brother and rival, Carloman. If true, this likely would have made Turpin less of an ally of Charlemagne than the *chansons de geste* came to portray. *The Song of Roland* depicts Turpin as a fierce, militant cleric who strikes down four hundred foes at Roncesvalles Pass before falling there alongside Roland. The Turpin of *The Fae Dealings* is obviously based more on the legendary archbishop than his historical counterpart.

In the epic poems, Bradamante is often portrayed as both the sister of Renaud and the cousin of Roland. Not all the *chansons de geste* are consistent about her lineage, however, and for the sake of this story, I decided to keep her bloodline separate from that of Maugis and his two cousins.

As for the tale of the paladins' mission, it is entirely fictional. Although, as I mentioned before, it is a crucial part of the backstory in both *Enoch's Device* and *The Key to the Abyss*. If you've read those books, you'll know where the paladins are heading—and just how dangerous their mission is about to become. But even if you haven't, I plan to continue their journey and explore more of the story of Angelica and Maugis too.

After all, there are many more legends to reimagine!

THE ADVENTURE CONTINUES WITH BOOK I OF *THE DRAGON-MYTH Cycle, Enoch's Device...*

FREE SHORT STORY

Get a free copy of *Mava's Echo: A Short Story of Celtic Myth and Magic!*

The promise of gold lures an Irish chieftain and Mava, his strong-willed wife, to an ancient ringfort. But when a banshee's cry echoes from the ruins, they are warned to turn back. Or at least one of them is going to die...

Get your free short story instantly by joining my author newsletter here: authorjosephfinley.com/free-short-story

By signing up, you'll also be the first to know about new releases and special offers.

BOOKS BY JOSEPH FINLEY

ABOUT THE AUTHOR

Joseph Finley is a writer of historical fantasy fiction. Following a tour as an officer in the U.S. Navy Judge Advocate General's Corps, he returned to Atlanta where he lives with his wife, daughter, and two mischievous rescue dogs. A lifelong love of medieval history, vintage fantasy, and historical mysteries helped inspire his writing, along with a penchant for European travel. Joseph is a member of the Science Fiction and Fantasy Writers of America, and posts frequently about historical and fantasy fiction on his blog. He can be found most nights enjoying a hearty glass of wine, and in the wee hours of most mornings surrounded by history books and plugging away on his next story.

To receive a **free short story**, as well as updates on Joseph's next novel and special offers, join his Reader List by signing up **here** or at his website, below:

www.authorjosephfinley.com

Lastly, if you enjoyed this book, please consider leaving a review (even if it's only a line or two) at Amazon or Goodreads. Word-of-mouth is essential to an author's success, so your input is greatly appreciated!

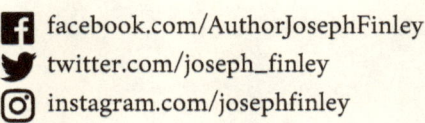

facebook.com/AuthorJosephFinley
twitter.com/joseph_finley
instagram.com/josephfinley

www.ingramcontent.com/pod-product-compliance
Lightning Source LLC
Chambersburg PA
CBHW020744130626
46554CB00006B/2141